WILLY VLAUTIN

The Night Always Comes

faber

First published in 2021
by Faber & Faber Limited
Bloomsbury House
74–77 Great Russell Street
London WC1B 3DA

Typeset by Typo•glyphix, Burton-on-Trent, DE14 3HE
Printed in the UK by CPI Group (UK) Ltd, Croydon, CR0 4YY

The right of Willy Vlautin to be identified as author of this work
has been asserted in accordance with Section 77 of the Copyright,
Designs and Patents Act 1988

Extract from *The Treasure of the Sierra Madre* by B. Traven
© The B. Traven Estate: Maria Eugenia Montes de Oca Luján
and Irene Pomar Montes de Oca

*Every effort has been made to trace copyright holders and to obtain
permission for the use of copyright material. The publisher would be
pleased to rectify any omissions that are brought to its attention
at the earliest opportunity*

A CIP record for this book
is available from the British Library

ISBN 978-0-571-36191-5

FSC
www.fsc.org
MIX
Paper from
responsible sources
FSC® C020471

2 4 6 8 10 9 7 5 3 1

For the Portland that let a hard-living
house painter buy his own house

The point is that you can't be too greedy.
        —The 45th President of the United States of America

Gold is a very devilish sort of thing, believe me, boys. In
the first place, it changes your character entirely. When you
have it your soul is no longer the same as it was before . . .
You cease to distinguish between right and wrong. You can
no longer see clearly what is good and what is bad.
        —B. Traven, *The Treasure of the Sierra Madre*

1

Kenny had his hands around her ankle and began pulling her from the bed. A small lamp on the dresser was the only light in the room as he stood over her in his Superman T-shirt and pyjama bottoms. A portable radiant heater in the middle of the room gave off little warmth and it was winter, and his breath came out in small disappearing clouds.

Lynette woke suddenly and looked at the clock on the nightstand: 3 a.m. 'I get to sleep for fifteen more minutes. So please don't touch me or say anything until then.' She was thirty years old and got out of bed in ten-year-old sweats and wool socks, shut off the light on the dresser, and climbed back under the covers.

In the darkness his breathing grew louder.

'Go back upstairs,' she cried.

He began to whimper.

'Please,' she begged, but he didn't stop. It only became worse so she turned on the bedside lamp next to the alarm clock and looked at him. 'Jesus, don't start crying. It's too early and I'm exhausted and you know I'm mean when I'm exhausted. But even so you come down here every morning when you know you're not supposed to. Every morning it's the same thing.'

His face was red and tears ran from his eyes.

'Come on, stop it. I'm too tired for you to cry. You have to let me sleep.' She pulled the sheet, the two blankets and the comforter over her head. From underneath she said,

'You know the rules. You have to wait until the alarm goes off. That's the rule. When the alarm goes off you can come down. Not before. I've told you a million times. Just wait at the top of the stairs. Wait until you hear the alarm. We've talked about this over and over. Don't you remember?'

Her brother shook his head.

'You remember – I can tell just by your breathing.'

Kenny shook his head but began to smile. He grabbed at her leg through the bedding.

She pulled the covers back. 'Jesus, alright, okay, you win. But I'll only get up if you brush your teeth.'

He shook his head.

'Your breath could kill somebody. Even in the cold I can smell it. Put on the clean sweats I set out, brush your teeth and let me get ready for work. Okay?'

He shook his head.

'In five seconds I'm gonna get mad again.' She pointed to the stairs and finally her brother headed for them. She stayed in bed and watched as he walked away. He was thirty-two years old and gaining more weight each year. His body had become a pear. He was five feet ten inches tall and waddled when he walked, with thinning brown hair and a growing bald spot on the crown of his head. He had monthly seizures and couldn't talk but for sounds that came out almost like words. The doctors said that he had the mind of a three-year-old. Sometimes that seemed too low and other times too high.

He lumbered up the stairs and she got out of bed.

★

2

The foundation of the house had been poured in 1922 using faulty concrete. During the winter rains it leaked in a half-dozen places. Over the years small sections of concrete wall had grown soft, the cement beginning to crumble. Their first landlord had hired a company to patch the foundation, but he had died and his son, who lived on the coast near Astoria, had inherited the house. He hadn't raised the rent in eleven years on the understanding that they wouldn't call him for repairs. So they didn't, and the basement was left to leak.

Across the room from Lynette's bed was a working washing machine and dryer, a 1960s oil furnace, a concrete utility sink and shelves filled with boxes. When she was in high school she had painted her section of the floor dark blue and the walls light blue. She had hung posters. The room now had the same coloured floor but the posters were gone and the walls were white and bare. She had her mother's old full-sized bed, a dresser that came with the house, two of its legs now bricks, and a six-foot-long wooden pole that was nailed to the ceiling where she hung her clothes.

She put on her work pants and a navy-blue T-shirt that read *9th Street Bakery* in cream-coloured ink. In a backpack she put a change of clothes and her classwork and went upstairs to find her mother in the living room asleep on the couch, the TV still on. Lynette shut it off and went to the bathroom. The toilet hadn't been flushed and used toilet paper was on the floor. She picked it up and flushed it. She cleaned the seat, used it herself, then washed her face and brushed her teeth and hair.

Her brother was sitting on his bed dressed in matching red Portland Trail Blazers sweatpants and hoodie. His walls were covered in twenty-year-old Portland Trail Blazers, Winterhawks and Beavers posters. He slept on a twin bed in the corner of the room; a black, red and white Trail Blazers comforter covered it. A Superman lamp sat on a dresser. Two Superman nightlights were plugged into wall sockets.

'Shoes,' Lynette said.

Kenny smiled but shook his head.

'Don't play around. We're gonna be late if you do.' She picked up two pairs of sweats off the floor, smelled them and then folded them and set them on top of his dresser. She found his red-and-black Blazers knit cap and put it on his head. 'Don't take it off. That's an order. We can't keep losing hats.' She looked on the floor for socks, found two, smelled them, and put them on his feet. 'Tomorrow we cut your nails.'

He shook his head.

'They're getting gross. Let me see what you put in your backpack.'

He wrapped his arms around it.

'Come on, Kenny.'

He shook his head.

'Alright, then suit yourself. Let's just get our shoes and go.'

She grabbed his hand and they walked out to the main room to find the TV on again.

'Can't sleep?' asked Lynette.

Their mother looked at them from the couch. She was

covered in a leopard-print electric blanket. 'I always forget how early you get up.' She reached to the coffee table, found her cigarettes, a lighter, and lit one as she lay on her back. 'What time you bringing him home?'

'I get out of class at two. I'll be here by two fifteen and then I have my shift at three thirty. I called Sally but she can't watch him. I figure I'll lock him in his room with a movie. He'll be alone for just over two hours if you come home right after you get off.'

Her mother coughed. 'I might not go to work today.'

'You sick?'

She nodded and a trail of smoke left her mouth.

'Then you keep him.'

Her mother slowly shook her head. 'Nah . . . I'm just wishing. I have to go in.' She put the cigarette in an ashtray, sat up and said, 'Come here, Superman.' She patted the couch and Kenny came to her. 'Be a good boy today. Do what your sister says.' She kissed him on the forehead and then lay back down.

★

Lynette locked the front door and, on the porch, zipped up her coat and then Kenny's. Their house behind them was shingled with grey asbestos siding and the single-paned windows were original and painted white. It was a thousand square feet and across the road was a concrete wall blocking the sight and some of the traffic noise of Interstate 5.

It was January and raining and forty-one degrees when Lynette and her brother walked across the lawn to her

5

1992 red Nissan Sentra. She opened the passenger-side door and Kenny got in. She put on his seatbelt and walked around to the driver's side. The car started on the second try but the heater hadn't worked in a year and their breath fogged the inside windows. She drove with one hand on the wheel and the other holding a rag she used to wipe the condensation and steam from the windshield.

'There's a red car passing us,' Lynette said half-heartedly. 'Do you see it?'

Kenny smiled and pointed at it.

She put her hand on his arm and squeezed. 'Maybe seeing your favourite-coloured car so early means we'll have a lucky day.'

They crossed the Fremont Bridge in the still black of night and the radio played and the rain fell. Kenny looked out the window at the blurred lights of Portland and Lynette leaned into the driver's-side door and sighed.

The 9th Street Bakery had sold its employee parking lot two years earlier. In its place was a half-built ten-storey condominium building. Lynette was now forced to park on the street. It was free until 8 a.m. and then she paid by the hour until she left at noon. That morning she found a spot directly across from the bakery and she held Kenny's hand and carried his backpack as they walked across the street. The bakery was closed but a side door was left open and they went through a storage area to the break room, where she sat her brother at a table with her phone, a sheet of butcher paper and a box of crayons.

'Don't leave this room unless you have to use the bathroom,' she said, 'but find me first. And don't wait too long like you did yesterday because I forgot to bring you a change of clothes. So hold it and then find me, okay? Hold it and then find me. You know where I'll be. I won't be mad. I really won't. I'll be happy if you let me know. Understand?'

He nodded and she started the movie *Toy Story* on her phone and left. She clocked in at 4 a.m. and began her shift as the pastry lead, taking trays of croissants and Danishes from the proofer and putting them in the oven. Every hour she would go into the break room and check on her brother. She would walk him to the bathroom and try to get him to use it, or start another movie on her phone. At 7 a.m. she took her first real break and sat with him.

Kenny pointed to the window outside.

'I don't have time today but I'll let you walk around the block. If I do, though, I have to keep the phone.'

Kenny shook his head.

'You can't have both, you know that. Choose one.'

Kenny handed her the phone.

'Don't stop unless you see Karen waiting outside Fuller's, okay? If you see her and she invites you in then you can go. But if she's not there don't let any bums talk to you, especially if they're young. And if they have dogs, well, then just turn around and come back here. Those kinds of dogs don't want to be petted. Remember what happened last time? That bite really hurt and you were really scared. So no petting dogs. Especially a bum's dog.'

She put his coat and hat on and kissed him, then unlocked the side door and watched him head down the sidewalk. She got a cup of coffee, sat at the break table and called Fuller's Diner.

'It's Lynette. Kenny's coming. Can you give him just one pancake and two scrambled eggs? The scrambled eggs have to be sitting on top of the pancake or he won't eat them. And remember to just pour the syrup – he'll use the whole thing if you let him. If he gets upset just tell him I can see if he uses too much. That I see him from where I am . . . I know, same old story . . . And don't leave the syrup anywhere near him. I've seen him drink a whole bottle . . . I know, it's disgusting . . . Thanks again. I'll bring you over some treats when I get off. And I'll pay you for this week too . . . Text me when he's leaving, okay?'

She hung up, took a sip of coffee, let her head fall to the table and closed her eyes. Her break ended and she went back to work. More employees arrived, including the owner, and the bakery opened. She worked for forty-five minutes more, then received a text and went outside to meet her brother on the street.

'You ready for your nap?'

Kenny nodded.

They came to her car, she opened the passenger-side door and Kenny got in. From the back seat she took a sleeping bag and covered him with it. 'The owner's here now so you can't come in. Just sleep, okay? I'll check on you my last break and we'll go to Fuller's and use their toilet. We only have four more hours now. We're almost there. I'll come check on you every chance I can. If it's an emergency and you have to go to the bathroom just get out of the car and come find me. That's only for an emergency, though. And remember not to open the door for anyone. Not anyone, alright? Not even if they look friendly or if they're wearing hard hats. Not even if they look like policemen and knock on the door and smile. Okay? And I saw a red car when I was walking toward Fuller's. So that's two. Pretty exciting. Let me know if you see any more.' He put his arms out and hugged her and wouldn't let her go. 'Come on, quit playing. I gotta work.' He let go of her and she said, 'Okay, Superman, it's time to sleep. That's an order.' She kissed him and locked the car door.

Three more times she checked on him and always he was asleep. She clocked out at noon, changed her clothes in the women's bathroom, and left with two ham-and-cheese sandwiches, a coffee, an orange soda and two pains aux raisins.

★

The day was dark and the rain continued and she drove through the Pearl District toward the freeway. Twenty years ago the area had mostly been deserted warehouses; now high-end lofts and stores, restaurants and condominiums stood in their place. With her right hand she wiped the rag across the inside of the windshield and they crossed the Broadway Bridge to the east side and headed north on Williams. There were more new apartment buildings and restaurants and bars. Lynette couldn't even remember what had been on Williams or Mississippi five years before. Twenty years ago her mother would have never set foot on Mississippi and now they walked the street on weekends. They looked in shops at clothes and shoes they could never afford and at menus in restaurants they would never go in. Their family place, a Greek diner on North Skidmore named The Overlook, had just closed. They had eaten there twice a month for twenty-five years. The owners had been offered more and more money for the land and eventually it was enough that they sold. The restaurant was torn down and construction on an apartment building had begun.

At Portland Community College, Lynette parked and they got out. She ate her sandwich while they walked through campus. In a lecture room inside Cascade Hall they sat in the back at the end of a long table. She unwrapped Kenny's sandwich and opened his soda while seventy-five students arrived for 'Intro to Accounting'.

She leaned over and whispered in his ear: 'Remember we have to be quiet, okay? That means not a peep. No farting either.'

But twenty minutes into the lecture Kenny started farting. Nearby students gave them looks and Kenny pulled on Lynette's shirt.

'Is it an emergency or can you wait?' she asked.

Kenny looked worried, he tugged at her again, so she walked him out of the lecture hall to the men's bathroom. She led him into a stall and then leaned against a sink outside it and waited.

'Remember to pull down your pants and underwear. Remember to sit before you go. Pants, underwear, sit, and go.'

A student came in and used the urinal and left. Five minutes passed.

'Come on, I have to hear at least some of the lecture. Are you almost done?' She opened the stall door to see him smiling and still sitting.

'Come on, don't play. Go and wipe.' She closed the stall door, waited two minutes more, and opened it again. 'You done?'

Kenny shook his head and again smiled.

'Alright, wipe one more time for me.'

Kenny took a handful of toilet paper from the roll and wiped himself.

'Alright, underwear and then your pants.'

Kenny pulled up his underwear, then the sweats, and walked out of the stall. She checked the toilet, flushed it, helped him wash his hands and they went back to class.

The teacher, a middle-aged man from India, had a strong accent and a weak voice that wasn't quite loud enough to hear from where she was sitting, and the room was warm and she grew tired. Her brother played with her phone and she began to fall asleep. When the class ended, a teaching assistant stood near the exit handing back the first exam of the term. She had passed but with seventy-three per cent. For a week straight she had studied and yet she'd only managed a seventy-three.

They walked back through campus to her car. The windows fogged as they sat in the parking lot and tears welled in Lynette's eyes. She slumped back in her seat. Kenny pulled on her coat. 'Don't worry,' she whispered. 'I'm just tired. Just hold my hand for a little.' She put her hand on his hand. 'I always wished I was smart but I guess I have to face the fact I'm just not. I only need a minute, okay? Just give me a minute.' She closed her eyes. A song was playing on the radio and she gave herself until it was over, then opened them and tried to smile. 'Alright,' she said, 'I'm all better now. Let's get you home.'

3

In the carport to the right of the house was a car Lynette had never seen, a white Toyota Avalon Limited. It had no licence plate, only a placard that said *Toyota of Portland*, and taped to the rear windshield was a white trip permit. Lynette parked on the street, got out, opened the passenger-side door for Kenny and helped him from the car. They walked across the front lawn and she stopped and looked inside the Toyota. The seats were black leather and a clear plastic liner covered the carpeted floor. It was brand new.

Inside the house the curtains were shut and the lights were off. Their mother was lying on the couch underneath the electric blanket, watching TV. She sat up when they came in. 'Come here and kiss your mother,' she said to Kenny. He walked slowly toward her and her hands shook slightly as she lit a cigarette, put it in her mouth and took hold of his arm. 'Sit next to me.' She patted the couch with her free hand. 'Sit right next to Mommy.'

Kenny only shook his head.

'Once in a while you have to do what somebody else wants and not what you want. So sit.' She squeezed his wrist as hard as she could and pulled him down to her. He moaned but sat.

Lynette set her purse and keys on a table near the front door. 'Whose car is that?'

Her mother didn't answer.

'Jesus, it's so awful out today.' Lynette walked into the living room. 'I don't know why you have it so dark in here all the time. Do you mind if I turn up the heat, at least for a little bit? I can't seem to get warm today.'

'Sure,' her mother said.

Lynette turned the thermostat up to sixty-eight. 'So whose car is that? It's really nice. Is it Cheryl's? Did yours break down?'

Her mother had the cigarette in her left hand and kept her right hand around Kenny's wrist. Her eyes were on the TV and her voice came out so quiet it was barely audible. 'It's mine.'

Lynette laughed. 'It's yours? I bet.'

Her mother's voice grew louder but now it was shaking. 'I . . . I bought it.'

Lynette looked at her, suddenly worried. 'What do you mean, you bought it? You mean you bought a car today? While I was gone? You didn't go to work like you said, you just bought a brand-new car?'

Her mother was fifty-seven years old and overweight by forty pounds. She had dyed brown hair and was dressed in her work clothes, a black suit with a cream-coloured blouse. On her feet were thick wool socks. She put the electric blanket over Kenny's legs, moved closer to him and kept her hand tight around his wrist. 'I didn't tell you because I knew you'd get upset. But I've been looking to get a new car for a long time, you know that, and those guys at Toyota of Portland are nice. They're not slimy at all. So I set up an appointment and they had the one I wanted. I didn't even have to put money down, not a cent, and my payments aren't as bad as you'd think. They even gave me fifteen hundred for the Saturn and as you know that car was a death trap. The brakes were going out and it didn't steer right. It needed new tyres too. The guys at Schwab said I shouldn't even be driving it.'

'How much was it?'

'It was a good deal.'

'How much?'

'With everything and the better warranty, thirty-nine thousand.'

Lynette sat on a wooden chair next to the front door. She covered her face with her hands and her heart began racing. 'I'm really confused . . . We're supposed to sign the papers on the house next week. Is it going to screw up the loan? Did you think about the loan?'

Her mother shook her head. 'I remember when he wanted us to buy it for ninety thousand and now he wants three hundred? He has a lot of fucking nerve.'

'It was fifteen years ago he said ninety. That was a long time ago. And he's selling it to us for two hundred and eighty. He's taking twenty thousand dollars off what it's going to be listed at if he puts it on the market. Plus we're not going through realtors so we're saving even more. It's a really good deal and you know it. I told you just last week that the blue house down the street sold for four hundred.'

'That place is a hell of a lot nicer and not on the freeway.'

'I know but still . . . Jesus, why would you buy a car today?'

'I've wanted a new one for a long time. So finally, I just bought one.'

'That's it? You didn't think about how it'll affect us getting the house?'

Her mother didn't answer. Kenny wanted to get up from the couch but she wouldn't let him.

'Don't you want to still buy the house?' asked Lynette.

Again her mother remained silent.

'You know if we don't buy it, he'll just sell it to someone else, right? And you know as well as me we can't afford any other house around here. We'll have to get an apartment and the apartment's gonna cost more than the mortgage. Even a crappy two-bedroom apartment around here is fifteen hundred and that's if we're lucky. We only pay eight hundred now. If we buy this place we'll have to pay around twelve hundred a month, but still that's less. That's three hundred dollars less a month than any apartment and we'll finally own something.'

Her mother knocked the ash from her cigarette into an empty Coke can. 'He talks an awful lot but, believe me, he won't really sell. He's said all this shit before.'

'But this time is different and you know it. He already agreed to sell it to us. If we back out he'll just put it on the market. He had the realtor come by. She took pictures and everything. You were here when she did the walk-through. He's tired and old and wants to sell.'

Her mother's hand shook as she picked up a Starbucks cup off the coffee table. Kenny grabbed for it but missed. 'Don't!' she yelled at him.

'Mr Claremont's been nice to us,' said Lynette. 'He's trying to help us.'

'Help us? This house is a shithole and he hasn't fixed

anything in years. How can that be nice?'

'That's not fair.'

'Well, it's true.'

Lynette closed her eyes. Her heart was beating so fast she thought she might vomit. 'We decided not to tell him about anything wrong 'cause we were scared he'd start raising the rent like everyone else. So we didn't call him and he never raised the rent. You know that, and it worked. How can he be an asshole for that? Bonnie's rent has nearly doubled in the last five years. Even next door they raised it by four hundred dollars and that place is worse than ours . . . He's not bad. He's just seventy-five years old and doesn't care about this place and he doesn't need the money. He wants us to have this house. That's why he's giving us first shot and giving us a good deal.'

'Then you buy it,' her mother said, and let out a rough laugh.

Tears suddenly leaked down Lynette's face. 'You know I can't get a loan,' she said in a heartbroken voice. 'We've gone over this a hundred times. I just don't understand why you're doing this right now. I've worked so hard to get the down payment.'

'You don't have eighty thousand dollars.'

'I do and you know it. I've showed you my bank account. It's in there.'

Her mother set down the Starbucks cup. 'But it's me that's gonna be handcuffed to the loan.'

'So that's it?'

Her mother didn't say anything.

'We're trying to build something,' said Lynette. 'We're

trying to make sure we have a good future. This is a great deal. I like it here and Kenny likes it here and everyone in the neighbourhood knows him and looks out for him.'

Her mother put out her cigarette. 'I'm fifty-seven years old and I still buy my clothes at Goodwill. It's a little late for me to care about building a future. And Kenny will be fine anywhere.' She kept her eyes on the TV and coughed. 'You don't know what it's like. Other women my age are going on vacations with their grandkids, they're talking about retirement plans and investments. Me, I haven't taken a vacation since the time we went to San Francisco and that was over fifteen years ago. I'll have to work at Fred Meyer until I drop dead. I'll never get to retire and that's just a goddamn fact. So lately I've been asking myself, why do I have to sacrifice even more than I already have? Why do I have to have a debt hanging over me for the rest of my life? Haven't I given enough? I mean, why can't I have something nice for a change? Just for me, just once. I drove that piece-of-shit Saturn for seventeen years. And day after day everyone on the road saw me for what I am, a middle-aged, overweight fatso loser.'

'But it's just a car,' said Lynette. 'You only drive it to work and back. Cars don't mean anything.'

'That's what you think,' said her mother. 'But you don't know. Things like that mean something.'

'I don't think they do. Not really.'

'I've worked at that Fred Meyer Jewelers for so long and all I have to show for it is being able to get a two-hundred-thousand-dollar loan on an overpriced, falling-down, piece-of-shit house?'

'But we're getting security,' said Lynette. 'We'll finally have something of our own that we can fix up, that we won't ever get kicked out of. Because if we get kicked out of this house, we're kicked out of the neighbourhood.'

Her mother took another drink from her Starbucks cup and Kenny again grabbed for it. 'Goddamn it, stop,' she snapped. 'I'm not in the mood.' She looked at Lynette. 'Don't you think I know that the house is really for you? That it has nothing to do with me?'

'Jesus,' cried Lynette. 'Why would you say that? Have you gone insane?'

'Me, insane?' She let out another mean laugh. 'I'm not the one with the mental problems. I'm not the one who's been committed.'

Lynette sprung up from the chair. Her fists clenched and her face turned red. 'Why would you say that right now?' she yelled. 'For fuck's sake, why would you throw that at me right now?'

Her mother looked at Kenny and leaned into him. 'Here we go,' she whispered. 'I knew this part would come. Hang on tight.' She let go of his wrist, just for a moment, and reached for her pack of cigarettes. Her hands shook violently as she lit one. She kept her eyes on the TV while she did it and Kenny grabbed for the Starbucks cup but knocked it over.

4

Kenny screamed when he saw what he'd done and jumped up from the couch and began pacing around the room. Lynette went to him and stopped him and took his hand. 'It's okay, Superman,' she said gently. 'I'm sorry, buddy, I didn't mean to yell. We're just talking about important things and I got carried away. And that carpet's old and the coffee will come out. It's no big deal. We're all okay so come on, we'll go to your room and set up a movie.'

Kenny shook his head and tears streamed down his face.

'Don't worry, baby,' their mother said. 'Everything's okay. Just go with your sister.'

Lynette went to the kitchen. In a locked cupboard was a box of Pop-Tarts. She put a single one on a plate, grabbed a kitchen towel and went back to the living room. She threw the towel to her mother.

'How about a Pop-Tart?' she asked Kenny.

He quit crying as soon as he saw it and Lynette grabbed his hand and took him to his room. She turned on a box heater, helped him off with his shoes and he sat on the bed while he ate. She shut the bedroom door, sat down next to him and began to sob.

Kenny tugged on her sweater.

'Don't worry,' she whispered. 'I'll be okay in a minute. I'm sorry I yelled. I didn't mean to. It just came out.'

A colour TV sat on a desk in front of the bed. She started *WALL-E* on the DVD player, placed headphones on Kenny and then sat back down on the bed next to him. She put her arm around him but he only pushed her away.

★

Their mother was still on the couch when Lynette returned twenty minutes later. No cigarette was burning and the leopard-print electric blanket covered her up to her neck.

Lynette sat in the same chair by the door and looked at her. 'I didn't mean to yell. I'm sorry. This is just a lot to process. You've really blindsided me . . . Look, I know you hate this place and you have a lot of reasons to. A lot. But I'm telling you if we don't buy it we'll have to move and we won't get to decide where we live. We'll never find a house around here, that's for sure. There's a good chance we'll end up in Gresham or off Columbia in some sorta apartment complex. I know we don't want that. We both grew up in this area and I know we both want to stay. And remember, everyone I've asked says we should buy it. The accountant at the bakery looked it over and said we should. I also asked Joe who owns The Dutchman. He said we'd be crazy not to buy it. I even asked my accounting professor. Every single one of them said we should do it. And once we buy it we can fix it up. We won't let stuff slide just because we don't want to call the landlord. You'll be surprised how nice I can get this place. Pretty soon it won't be an old piece of shit, it'll be something different. It'll be ours.'

The room was so dark Lynette couldn't see if her mother's eyes were open or closed. The sound of the TV was the only noise in the room. She waited for her mother to reply but she didn't.

'You have to tell me what's really going on,' said Lynette. 'I'm having trouble breathing. I'm really scared and I don't understand what you're doing. We've had this plan for three years and now a week before we're supposed to sign the papers you buy a fancy car and say you don't want the house.'

'I'm too tired to talk about this,' whispered her mother.

'If it's about the car we'll get you a decent one later on. I promise. But the house is the thing we should be worried about. You know I can't get a loan or I'd do it. You know I've tried. The job at the bakery doesn't pay enough and The Dutchman is mostly just tip money, and I can't get more hours, I've tried. I paid off my credit cards but they'd all gone to collections by then. I have bad credit. On paper I look like shit. I've apologized a million times for that. You know I have. But I have the cash for the down payment. I really do.'

'How did you get eighty thousand dollars?'

'I just got it.'

Her mother sighed and her voice quavered. 'Why is everything always put on me?'

'I know it seems like it is, but it's not,' said Lynette. 'Buying this house will make it less on you. We'll have security, we won't answer to anybody and we won't get kicked out. And I'll do all the work. I'll make this place really nice.'

Her mother sat up and the electric blanket fell to her lap. She took a cigarette from the pack on the coffee table and lit it. 'You can say I'm the worst mother in the world because of this . . . Maybe I am. And you can blame me for everything that's ever happened to you. Maybe you should. But I give and give and what do I ever get? I'm not trying to sound horrible. I'm just being honest. What do I get? Well, I'll tell you what. I'll be handcuffed to a loan on an overpriced falling-down house. And it's a house I hate. A house that you've tried to kill yourself in, a house that's been like a prison since Kenny was born, a house that your father abandoned us in . . . So I said to myself, Doreen, you deserve something nice for a change. You deserve to treat yourself. Just this one time. Just one time in your life.'

Lynette got up from the chair and started to pace the room.

'You're gonna go nuts now and throw things,' said her mother. 'I can feel it.'

'I'm not,' Lynette said, shaking her head. 'I'm not like that any more and you know it. I've worked really, really hard. I'm not like that . . . Why do you keep bringing up the way I used to be?'

'Because the way you used to be is still in you. I can see it right now trying to get out. You say you've changed but I don't think you have. Because people don't change. That's one thing I've learned in this life. And let me tell you, no one likes being pushed around and threatened. They don't and that's what you've been doing to me about this house. It's probably why you can't keep a boyfriend.'

'I don't want a boyfriend.'

'You sure wanted Jack.'

'Jesus, why would you bring him up right now?' Lynette cried. 'Why are you being so mean to me?'

Her mother wouldn't look at her; she only knocked the ash from her cigarette into the Coke can and sighed. 'I'm sorry, I shouldn't have said that. I guess I'm upset too.'

'Don't ever bring him up. You have no right to and I'll fall apart if I think about that. You saying that is being really awful to me.'

Her mother nodded.

Lynette sat back down and rested her elbows on her knees. They sat for a minute in silence and then she said, 'Remember when we went to that open house at that new apartment building on Mississippi?'

'I remember.'

'We knew then. You're the one who said it to me. "If he sells we're fucked." Twenty-eight hundred dollars for a three-bedroom apartment. Remember? We ate lunch at Lung Fung afterward. We talked about it. We were both really worried. I thought we came up with a good plan then.'

'It wasn't my plan.'

'You didn't say no. You never once said no.'

'If I would have, you'd have just yelled at me.'

'That's unfair,' said Lynette. 'You have to stop talking like that.'

Her mother looked at her. 'It's gonna hurt what I'm gonna say, Lynette, but it's true. When someone's been as mean as you, the other things don't come back. You think they will but they don't because right behind the new niceness and new smile is the old yelling and old anger.'

Lynette nodded. She whispered, 'I know you've put up with a lot. I'm not denying that. That's why I'm trying to make sure we get the house.'

'You ran away on me.'

'I know.'

'It almost killed me.'

'That was fourteen years ago and I've apologized a thousand times. What's the point of bringing it up now?'

Her mother took a long pull from the cigarette, exhaled and coughed. 'I didn't know where you really were for eleven months. You only called once in a while to let me know you were alive. You wouldn't tell me anything. Hardly nothing. I only got updates from Marsha when you'd visit Kenny. There I was struggling just to keep us afloat, keep my job and keep Kenny in one piece, and you, my sixteen-year-old daughter, had to run away.'

'I wasn't trying to be mean to you back then,' said Lynette. 'I was just mad and scared. There's a difference. I know it doesn't seem like a difference but I wasn't trying to be mean. That's not why I left when I did. I had to and you know why.'

Her mother got up off the couch, walked to the kitchen and unlocked the fridge. She took out a quart of chocolate milk and poured herself a glass, then came back to the couch, sat down and lit another cigarette even though one was still burning in the ashtray. 'I didn't know why you ran away and you can't say I did. So I'm not going to feel guilty about that. I'm not. I didn't know because you didn't tell me. All I did was come home one night and you were gone and I thought I was gonna die. I couldn't sleep for months. I had constant diarrhoea. I used to throw up at work. It was the worst time in my entire life. Worse than finding out about Kenny, worse than your father abandoning us. Worse than finding you bloody in bed after you came back and tried to kill yourself. Because it was the first time, and first times always hurt the worst.

'What you don't remember is how relieved I was when you came home. Just so grateful. Jesus, you have no idea. I thought, It's all over now. She's safe now. Little did I know it was just the start of the hard times. Just the beginning. Because you came home a different person. You weren't my Lynette any more. You were just a shell who was underweight, who had hives covering half her back, who wouldn't eat, who wouldn't go to school, who wouldn't take care of herself.'

She paused and took a drink of the chocolate milk. 'What you don't understand is that I've always been scraping by. Always. Your father never paid his full child support and you don't know how many times I called begging him for money. I begged him when I knew he cheated on me. I begged him even though, after the doctor said Kenny would never be right, he quit touching me. I was five months pregnant with you. He just quits touching me, quits kissing me, quits hugging me or being nice. Think how that makes me feel. And then he just leaves. You're four months old and I take you guys to Yakima to show you off to my aunt and uncle and when we come back all his things are gone. Even the TV and the microwave. A new mother and he takes the microwave. My fucking God . . . But even so, even though I hate him more than anyone in this world, I call him up and beg and beg and beg and I get the only job I know, waitressing. I put one foot in front of the other. And let me tell you, it's hard to do.'

Lynette rubbed her face with her hands and thought of her mom's old boyfriend. Randy in his boxers showing himself. Randy whispering to her. Randy taking her can of soda and drinking from it. Randy and her mom having sex. Randy asking the next morning if she'd heard it. Randy wanting to take her shopping or to the movies by herself. Randy walking into the bathroom before she put the lock on it so he couldn't get in.

'I know you've had it rough,' she said. 'But I didn't leave to be mean and you know it. I left because of him. Because your boyfriend broke the bathroom door down when I was in the tub and started grabbing for me . . . I still nearly throw up just thinking about it. If it wasn't for Kenny having a seizure, who knows what would have happened.'

'But I didn't know that!' cried her mother. 'Goddamn it, I didn't know. I mean, I lived with him for eight more months without knowing any of it. And I didn't know because you didn't tell me. You can't say it was my fault if I didn't have any idea.'

'I didn't tell you because I thought you liked him more than me. I thought if I told you, you'd kick me out. So I left 'cause I didn't want to be around him and I didn't want you to make me leave. I didn't want to hear you say you didn't want me.'

27

'Jesus,' cried her mother. 'Am I a monster? Is that what you really think of me? That I would do something like that? Push my own daughter out on the streets? I could have killed him once I found out. I really could have. And the son of a bitch didn't even deny it. He said he was in love with you. It made me so goddamn sick. It really did. It made me sick to the core . . . And this will sound horrible, will make me sound horrible, but part of me was jealous too. It hurt me that way because I was already getting fat and I knew he was getting tired of me. But let me tell you something, I was as good-looking as you are – I was, back before I had kids. Back before everything went wrong . . . When I was your age men stared at me all day long. Even in the grocery store, they couldn't keep their eyes off me. When I was a waitress they were all after me, all of them. For a lot of years I could have had any man I wanted. But . . . Regardless of how much I hated Randy for what he did, it was awful when he left. But not for the reasons you're thinking. I'm not a romantic. It had nothing to do with that. He was just the first man since your father who I liked who'd actually put up with Kenny. Who genuinely liked Kenny. I mean, that in itself was something. And he paid two thirds of the rent, took me out to dinner at least once a week, he bought us a lawnmower and paid for cable and groceries. He fixed the washing machine and gave me the Saturn. He bought us a dishwasher and installed it. Those things, they might seem stupid, but Jesus, they really helped.'

She took another drink of the chocolate milk. 'But it turns out all men are assholes. That's another thing I've learned in this life. Every single one of them except my father. But I think now my father was just different. He was just better than the rest of them. And Kenny, of course.'

She leaned over to the coffee table, took another cigarette from the pack and lit it. 'Kenny . . . You've said before that you think I've given up on him, given up on everything. Well, I've thought a lot about that and maybe I have, maybe that's true, but if I have it started that first time when you ran away and then came home wrecked. That first time broke me, you'll never have any idea how much, and I will say this, the second time after Jack left you, that time finished me off. That time was so awful. You know I used to tremble just going down the stairs? Did you know that? I'd say to myself, If she's not dead she's gonna yell at you. She's either gonna be laying there dead or she's gonna scream at you. Jesus, you could be mean.'

'I know I could,' Lynette said, hardly loud enough to hear. 'What do you want me to say? How many times do I have to apologize?'

'Apologies don't mean anything, don't you see? Because you've left scars and those scars don't just disappear because you haven't shown that side in a while. Just because you've gone to therapy and read books and tried to be different doesn't mean you really are. Because I know it's still in there. I can feel it. You don't think it is but it is. Look at my hands, they're shaking.'

She put out her hands.

'I know it's still there,' whispered Lynette. 'Don't you think I know that? But it doesn't come out now. It hasn't for a long time and it won't any more. That's what you don't understand. I'm getting better and I'm trying to make up for what I've done. That's why I'm trying to get us the house.'

Her mother held the cigarette in her lips and ran her hands through her hair. 'You know, after you came home the first time you never left the basement when I was home. Never. Like what had happened to you was my fault. Do you remember us fighting so I could wash your sheets? I had to beg you just to stand up.'

'Please stop talking about this stuff,' begged Lynette.

'The only light in all that gloom was when you'd eat waffles with Kenny. I'd make them and you two would eat them and then I'd run down and wash your bedding and your underwear and pyjamas and when I did I could hear you talking to him. You wouldn't talk to me, not a goddamn word, but you'd talk to him . . . You think I'm a bad mother but just seeing your pile of dirty under-wear on the floor made me so happy. Because a girl who changes her underwear must want to live. She must at least want to live a little bit. That's what kept me going. Sometimes I'd sit by the air return vent just to hear your voice. To hear you talk to Kenny. It was like Christmas to hear it. She'll make it, I said to myself, but then when I'd go back to the kitchen I'd try to join in and you'd fall silent. Like you were punishing me when I was trying so hard to help. You don't know how difficult it was to fight every day, to get up and try to help your daughter when you know your daughter hates you. Despises you . . . And then . . . And then, right when I think you're getting better, you try to kill yourself.'

'Why are you doing this?' Tears leaked down Lynette's face and she wanted to collapse to the floor.

Her mother took a drag from her cigarette and again looked at the TV. 'All I know is when I got home from work and saw you in your bed like that, with all that blood, I went into shock. Maybe I've never come out of that shock, I don't know . . . If I was smart I would have just put you in the car and driven you to the hospital myself. But I was so scared I could barely think . . . And then of course Kenny was having a fit 'cause I was having a fit. So I called 911. The whole thing cost me three thousand dollars 'cause of Fred Meyer's shitty insurance. A five-minute ride for three grand. Do you know how long it took me to pay that off? Four years. Four years to pay off three thousand dollars. Talk about not wanting to get out of bed.

'Do you know what I could have done with that money? I could have taken us on vacation. Can you imagine us on vacation? Can you see us going to Hawaii or even to Astoria for a weekend? With that money I could have bought new clothes instead of always going through the bins. You know, since Kenny I've only bought new underwear and new socks. For thirty-two years everything I've worn has been somebody else's hand-me-downs. That might not seem like much to you but it's something to me. It's something that just grates, that chips away at your confidence, at your belief in yourself.'

She got up again, poured herself another glass of chocolate milk, and then went back to the couch. 'And I'll never forget Child Services coming here. Sitting me down and asking me if I beat you. If I'm a drug addict.

If I'm an alcoholic. If you've been molested and why was it so cold in our house? And why were you in the basement? And had it been tested for radon? I didn't even know what radon was. They looked in our fridge and cupboards to see what kind of food we had. They checked to see if we had hot water. I mean, who the fuck do they think they are? And the whole time they're talking. Why this and why that? Like it was all my fault. Like everything in the world was my fault, not your father's for abandoning us. Not his fault that he only paid a third of his child support payments. Not his fault that he doesn't acknowledge Kenny as his son. And he never came to any of your school events. Not even softball and you were so good at that. I mean, my God. Did he visit you in the hospital?'

'No,' Lynette muttered. 'But you gotta stop. You're just trying to hurt me and it's working. Don't you think I hate myself enough? How many times have I said I'm sorry? For a third of my life I've apologized.'

Her mother took a pull from the cigarette then put it out. She coughed and looked at the TV. 'Child Services wanted you held for psychiatric evaluation. So I asked them, "If you take her somewhere, is it like *One Flew Over the Cuckoo's Nest*? Is it that bad? Will you give her shock therapy, will you give her a lobotomy? Please be honest and tell me if it's that bad because I don't know anything about this sort of thing." Well . . . They told me it wasn't. They swore on their lives they wouldn't do those things to you. But how did I know if I could trust them? And really, I had no one to talk to about it . . . But in the end I signed

32

the paper and I signed it because I couldn't get that image out of my mind. You in bed with all that blood all over you holding that box cutter. That's what did it. That's what made me sign the papers.'

'I needed help,' Lynette whispered. 'And you helped me. That's why I'm trying so hard now. Don't you see? To make up for everything I've done. To make things right. I haven't lost my temper in this house in over five years. I haven't thrown anything or lost control. I'm not saying I've been great but I'm not like I was. I've been working two jobs. I've done a lot of good things. I've gotten us a decent washer and dryer. I got us a new hot-water heater. We always have enough of everything and I'm more than pulling my weight with Kenny. I'm contributing and you know I am. So please, I'm begging you with everything I have, just stop bringing up the past. Stop punishing me. You can't change it, I can't change it. But we can have a good future. We can buy this house. That's something that'll change our lives. It will give us confidence. Mr Claremont is giving us our first real break. And I promise I'll stay and help. I will. But . . . But you have to stop picking on me and you have to take back the car.'

'I'm too tired,' her mother said, and she finished the chocolate milk and lay back down on the couch. 'I'm too tired to talk about this any more.'

'I know . . . But we have to figure it out. We have to take the car back.'

'I don't want to go back to the dealership,' her mother said. 'They'll think I'm an idiot. Just another dumb old fat lady who wanted to be a big shot and couldn't handle it.'

'Then I'll go with you,' said Lynette. 'I'll do all the talking. They'll understand. These things probably happen all the time.'

Her mother shook her head and covered herself with the electric blanket. 'I'm all talked out.' She grabbed the remote control and turned up the sound on the TV.

★

In the basement Lynette's hands shook so bad she could barely get undressed. She put her work clothes in a hamper by the dresser and stood naked and tried to breathe. She fell on the bed and stayed there for five minutes and then sat up, wiped the tears from her face, wrapped a towel around herself and walked back upstairs. In the bathroom she stood under the shower for ten minutes, exhausted, then got out, dried her hair, did her make-up and walked back to the living room with a towel around her. She sat in the same chair near the front door. 'Are you asleep?' she asked.

'No,' said her mother.

'I'm begging you. Please take the car back. I'll get you a new car. I promise. And I'll go with you and explain everything. You won't have to say a word. They'll understand. It's only been a few hours. But . . . But if you won't, if you really have to have it, then I just thought of something else. Maybe you can still get a loan for a hundred and sixty thousand. The amount less the car. I don't know what the bank thinks about things like that. Or maybe I can get a loan for forty thousand. You'd think, even with my bad credit, they'd give me that much. I hadn't thought of that before but maybe it could work. We could ask the bank. There's always a way. The more I think about it the more I don't think we're totally sunk. I just wasn't looking at it clearly. I just got upset. What do you think?'

Her mother didn't say anything.

'Did you hear me?'

Her mother pulled the leopard-print electric blanket to just under her neck. 'I can't,' she whispered.

'You can't what?'

'I can't live here the rest of my life.'

'Well, then what are we gonna do? Where are we gonna go?'

Her mother paused for a time and then said in a shaky voice, 'Maybe you should just do whatever you want.'

'Whatever I want? For three years I've been trying to get the down payment for this house and now in just one day you buy a car and change your mind?'

Her mother stared at the TV and said, 'Maybe . . . Maybe you should just live on your own.'

'On my own?' said Lynette.

'Yes.'

'Really?'

Her mother nodded.

Lynette put her hands over her face and sobbed. 'If I do go,' she said, 'then I'm taking Kenny. You haven't given a shit about him in a long time. And we'll leave and we'll never come back.'

'Well, then you can have him,' was all her mother said.

5

Lynette dressed for her shift at the bar, put a set of clothes together for afterward, and left the house. She was crying as she walked to her car. The day was already fading, the rain continued, and it took her six tries to get her car started. It was five miles to the cocktail lounge where the sign on the roof read *The Dutchman's Room* in red and white neon. Connected to the bar was a restaurant with windows that looked out onto the street. A handful of old people sat inside eating. The bar itself was to the left of the restaurant and had no windows, only a red front and side door and above each of them a white neon sign read *Good Times Await*. Inside was a classic lounge with a gas fireplace, red vinyl booths that lined the walls and a dozen small wooden tables in the centre. There were pictures and mementos from the Netherlands. Windmills were on the napkins, on the salt and pepper shakers, and engraved in gold on the glass mirror behind the bar.

In the break room Lynette put her coat and purse in her employee locker and sat for five minutes in a plastic chair next to a card table and closed her eyes. She then got up and went through a service door to the bar, where a sixty-eight-year-old woman stood making drinks.

'Hey, Shirley,' she said.

The old bartender looked at her red eyes and swollen face. 'You been crying all day, huh?'

Lynette shrugged.

'We'll talk about it when it slows down,' said Shirley, and squeezed Lynette's arm. The old woman had dyed red hair and red lipstick, and wore black polyester stretch pants, a sparkly gold top, thick black orthopaedic shoes and a pair of bifocal glasses. She had three gold rings on each hand and a black-and-gold choker around her neck.

Four construction workers came toward the bar, Lynette took their orders, and her shift began as The Dutchman grew crowded with after-work drinkers. The two women worked side by side non-stop until happy hour ended three hours later. Shirley clocked out, told Lynette to call her when she got off, and Lynette worked the bar alone.

Her father and two Central American men came in. All three wore painting clothes and flecks of white paint covered their hands and arms. Her father was fifty-eight years old and six feet two inches tall with thick black-and-grey hair. He was a handsome man with tired blue eyes and a veined alcoholic's face.

He leaned against the bar and said, 'Three Coors.'

Lynette took the bottles from the cooler and set them in front of him, and the three men went to a back corner booth and sat. He came back twice more for the same and then the Central American men left and he found a seat at the bar.

'You owe me for nine beers,' said Lynette.

'You ain't gonna charge your old man, are you?'

'You having another?'

He nodded.

'I'll get you that one but you have to pay for the nine.'

37

'Then I'll take a double Herradura neat and a Coors.'

Lynette shook her head but poured the drink and set it and the beer down. She took forty dollars from him and brought back the change. 'I've never seen those guys.'

Her father took a drink. 'They're new. I got four now, plus Gilberto. A big crew for me, but I'm booked six months in advance. I need all the help I can get. It's wild right now. Two days ago I bid a new construction condominium project off Hawthorne. Twelve units. They can't get a painting contractor to commit. I said I'd commit and more than doubled what I thought it would cost and the stupid fuckers took it. Without even blinking they took it. I should have tripled it. And my crew are good. They're all from El Salvador – they don't bitch, and really bust it.' He leaned over toward her and lowered his voice. 'And I don't deal with shit, taxes or nothing. I just give their pay to Gilberto. He hires and fires them and deals with it all. I just get the jobs.'

'Where do they live?'

Her father shrugged. 'Gilberto has some trailers on his property somewhere near Woodburn.'

'How much do you pay them?'

'Why do you care?'

Lynette shrugged.

'Shit, each guy only costs me twelve bucks an hour. They get driven up in Gilberto's van. It's a good deal for me and they're Gilberto's guys. I'm just subcontracting from him and he's legal. So it's more or less legit.'

'Twelve is barely minimum wage.'

Her father shrugged. 'I didn't ask them to sneak across the border. And look, I pay them every week. Every penny.

What they're actually getting is up to Gilberto. I have nothing to do with that. It's on him, not me.'

'You really believe that?'

Her father leaned back and smiled. 'I always forget you're a ball-buster.'

Lynette smiled. 'You haven't been here in like six months. You still living over on Woodstock?'

He took a drink of beer. 'Nah, the couple that owned that house sold it. They got four hundred and fifty grand for it . . . I'm living off 112th and Sandy. Half of a shitbox duplex. It's expensive as fuck, but it has three bedrooms and a full garage that I can spray in. It's not bad except we're next to the railroad tracks. All night long the trains go by. But I got earplugs, I don't really care. I've been drinking at a place called Katie's. You heard of it?'

'No.'

'I like the Woodstock area better but I'm making so much goddamn money right now I don't mind living in a dump for a while. Did I tell you I'm buying a boat? A guy I know is selling me his Alumaweld for twenty grand. It's got a great motor, less than two hundred hours on it.'

'A boat?'

He nodded. 'I got a lot of shit going on. Noreen's pregnant again too. Did I tell you that? You're gonna have another sister.'

'Aren't you a little old?'

He shrugged.

'That's what the world needs,' said Lynette. 'More kids with dads like you.'

He finished his beer and pointed to the empty bottle.

'You turned out alright. You got a job and you're the best-looking woman in this bar by a mile. I didn't do you so bad.'

Lynette brought him another beer and opened it. 'You were a piece-of-shit father at best and you know it.'

He nodded. 'Maybe, but I'm better this time around. I've been a good father to Hannah. She just turned four. You should stop by and see her. She needs to meet her big sister.'

Lynette laughed and a customer came to the bar and she went back to work. Ten minutes later it slowed and she returned to her father. 'How far along is she?'

'Who?'

'Your girlfriend, Noreen.'

'Seven months.'

'How you gonna afford that?'

'She's on the Oregon Health Plan. We ain't legally married.' He smiled. 'Right now I get free cable off our neighbour who doesn't know it, contractors are paying me any price I ask, my youngest daughter is cute as a button and my oldest daughter is a bartender at one of my favourite old bars.' He pointed to his glass. 'Speaking of which, Herradura, please.'

'You're gonna have to pay for this one.'

'Really?'

'Jesus,' she said, 'I can't give you free drinks all night.'

'Then make it Hornitos and pour like it's a triple.'

Lynette got him the drink and he put a twenty on the bar. 'I'm keeping the change,' she said.

'Then I want a Coors with it.'

She went to the cooler and came back with the beer.

He took both drinks and stood up. 'I'll see you around,' he said, and went to the back of the bar, sat at one of the video poker machines and put in a twenty-dollar bill. She didn't see him after that, and at seven the evening bartender came on and business had slowed enough that she clocked out and ate the dinner special in the employee break room. Afterward, in the kitchen bathroom, she gave herself a sink wash, changed her underwear and clothes, redid her make-up, combed her hair, put on her coat, and left.

6

It was now night and still the rain continued. The traffic was bumper to bumper as she made her way across the river to the Hotel deLuxe. When she was a kid it had been called The Mallory. Her aunt and uncle from Yakima would stay there and she, her mother and Kenny would meet them in the restaurant for breakfast or lunch. It had been a classic but fading landmark even then. Now developers had turned it into a modern high-end hotel.

The lobby was empty but for a single front-desk clerk who stood behind the counter. Lynette nodded to her, passed the closed restaurant and went into the hotel's only bar, the Driftwood Room, a small 1950s bar shaped like a kidney swimming pool. Banquette seating with small tables and chairs lined the elegant stained-wood walls. There was no one inside except the bartender and, in the back corner, a sixty-year-old pudgy bald man dressed in a blue suit.

'I've always liked that you're on time,' the pudgy man said to Lynette. 'I don't think you've been late once. No one else I know is like that, except for me, maybe.'

Lynette sat across from him and took off her scarf and coat. 'I hate being late,' she said, and smiled. 'I always have.'

'And I like that you picked this place. I think I came here once when I was in my twenties. I hadn't thought about it in years.' The man had a wedding ring on his left hand, an SAE fraternity ring on his right, and a white-gold Montblanc watch on his wrist. A small bowl of peanuts sat on the table and he took a handful of them.

'This is my favourite bar,' she said.

'You have good taste.'

'Jesus, it's freezing outside.'

'We'll get a drink in you,' he said, and waved to the bartender. Lynette ordered a hot toddy. 'I already got us a room,' the man continued. 'You know, I was surprised you called. You've never called me before.'

'I hope that's alright.'

He shrugged. 'It's good timing. My wife left for Scottsdale today and I had a meeting until six and my dinner plans got cancelled. I've never seen you not dress up either. I like it.'

She laughed. 'My rustic look.'

'Well, you look good rustic.'

The bartender came back with her drink and set it down. When he left she said, 'I've never stayed here but I heard they used to have beds that were shaped like hearts.'

He smiled and took a drink.

'They probably don't have those any more, huh?'

'Probably not,' he said. 'So why did you call me?'

She shrugged.

'You broke?'

'No,' she said. 'I'd never call you because of that.'

'Then what?'

'Can I ask you a serious question?'

'Is this why you called me?'

'Maybe. Not the only reason but I did want to ask you something.'

'About what?'

'Investing.'

'Investing?' He laughed. 'Investing what?'

'Money,' she said. 'I don't know anything about investing. Not really. I just have everything in the bank. But I want to know about it. Learn about it. I just don't know where to start and I thought of you.'

'I could get you a couple books.'

'I've been taking classes at PCC, but just about basic economics. I'm taking an accounting class now.'

'I didn't know that.'

She nodded. 'Could you help me more than with just book recommendations? Could I hire you?'

He moved in his chair and took a drink. 'The minimum my clients have is around five hundred.'

She leaned over and whispered, 'But I have around eighty thousand. Eighty thousand dollars is a lot more than five hundred.'

'Five hundred meaning five hundred thousand,' he said. 'And I only do that small of an amount if they're the friends or family of my real clients. I can't do much with eighty thousand.'

She slumped a little into the banquette. 'Five hundred thousand? Jesus, that's a small amount?'

'To a lot of people it's nothing. Have you seen those Edward Jones places?'

'Edward Jones?'

'They have offices everywhere. They have the green-

and-white signs. You'll see them in strip malls. Once you start looking, you'll see them.'

'What are they?'

'Investment places. You should go to one of them. They could help you invest the money.'

She took her purse, found a small notebook inside and wrote down *Edward Jones*. 'I have another question.'

He nodded.

'I'm trying to buy the house I live in with my mother and brother.'

'You live with your mother and brother?'

She nodded. 'It's on Missouri Street in North Portland. You know that area?'

'No,' he said.

'It's between Ainsworth and Killingsworth, right off I-5. Our house is right next to it. I have eighty thousand for a down payment, but I have bad credit. I was stupid with credit cards when I was younger. But what I'm trying to ask, what I'm trying to see is, and I know it's a lot to ask, but do you think your company could give me a loan for two hundred thousand?'

He leaned forward on his elbows. 'You want me to loan you two hundred thousand dollars?'

'No,' she said, 'not a personal loan. I don't mean like that. I mean a legitimate loan. I don't mean you personally. I would never ask that.' Her voice became more uncertain. 'Through your company. I know home loans are at about four per cent. I'd pay you more. Six or seven per cent. So maybe that will make up for my bad credit. The way I see it, if I default then you get my eighty thousand and the house. The house isn't much, but the second I buy it I'll start fixing it up. I'm getting a good deal on it, so really, if I do default, you'd still be getting a great deal. You'd make money on it no matter what happened. I know you would.'

'But I'm not a bank,' he said. He took another drink and watched as a middle-aged couple came in and sat at the bar.

'Then how do you think I could get the house?'

He shrugged.

'I know this is weird and we've never talked like this before, but I guess I'm sort of in a fix. My mom was supposed to get the loan, but now . . . well, everything has just sorta gone sideways on me and I'm trying to figure it out and I'm not the best at this sorta stuff. But I know you're really smart about it.'

The bartender came back. The man ordered a double Scotch and waited until it was sitting in front of him before he spoke again. 'I think I told you that I have three kids. My daughter is buying a house right now too, up on Council Crest. I have a son in grad school and one who's just starting out as a lawyer. They all ask things of me. Feels like almost every day I get a call. None of them seem happy. I don't know why they're not happy but they aren't. The calls I get aren't because they want to tell me something funny or to see how I'm doing. They're not calling to catch up. They just want money or help with something that involves money. I don't remember ever being like that, talking to my parents the way they talk to me. The way they complain . . . I have two brothers and we never demanded anything of our parents. We were just grateful for them. We respected them as much as we could, helped them when we could, because they'd helped us. I really tried to raise my kids the same way. But they're different. I don't know, maybe I'm just getting old. Or maybe I just failed them . . . My job demands of me all day long. I never get a happy call there either. Never. But that's work. Work's like that. It's always been like that. And they pay me. And my wife, well . . .' He took a sip and looked at Lynette. 'I see you because I don't want to think about any of that. I'm sorry but I don't want to know if you have a brother or live with your mother or what kind of car you drive or if you go to college. That's not saying I don't like you – I do. You're fun. But I pay you so we don't have to talk about the other shit. Because I'm tired of the other shit.'

Lynette nodded.

'Look, I don't mean to be an asshole but I can't mix these things. You're smart, you know why I can't. I can get you some books on general investing. Read them. They'll tell you what to do. Get a mutual fund at Edward Jones or at Charles Schwab. Ask for help there. They'll get you a plan together.'

Again she nodded.

'Did I upset you?'

'No,' she said, trying not to cry. 'I sorta figured but I thought I'd try.'

'You still want to go upstairs?'

'Sure,' she said, and forced herself to smile.

★

The room was dark but the TV was on. In bed he had lasted longer than he usually did. It took him nearly twenty minutes and he went limp three times. He had never gone limp before. Most times he wanted her to say things but tonight he wanted her silent. She was on top of him and the only noise in the room came from him grunting and her fake moans. They went on and on and on and then it was over. He spit out a half-grunt and then two louder grunts and then he stopped moving. He put his hands on her waist and gently asked her to move. He got up from the bed and walked to the bathroom with the rubber still on him. He put it in the toilet, flushed it, and got in the shower.

Sitting on the bed, Lynette began to cry. She had been with him twenty-four times and never once had she told him anything private. Always she made herself be in a good mood and forced herself not to talk too often. She never ate too much or drank too much. They did what he wanted to do and how he wanted to do it and there was comfort in that. A right and wrong way. A map. There was safety in it and she could be, at least for a night or two, somebody else.

She wasn't a professional, he was her first, and after their second meeting she'd started thinking of him as more than just money. There was a lightness between them and an ongoing flirtation. He said nice things to her and for no reason bought her gift cards. He'd flown her to San Francisco four separate times and they'd met at the Fairmont, where he got her a room. She had never in her life stayed in a nice hotel before. It wasn't that she loved him exactly, but she liked him and respected him. He was successful and he was decent to her. Never once had he abused her or looked down on her or degraded her. Because of that she had thought they were friends. That maybe, in a way, he was a sort of benefactor. That he had been looking out for her.

While he showered she fell apart on the bed and her anger welled. Anger at herself and anger at him. She wiped her eyes on the sheets and thought of his car. Still naked, she got up from the bed and went to the sport coat hanging on the chair by the desk. Inside the left pocket was a set of keys; she took off the car key, dropped it behind the desk and put the rest back. It wasn't that she wanted the car, she only wanted to hurt him in some way, and it was the only way she could think of right then. She gathered her clothes from the floor and he came out into the room. She stood next to the bed and couldn't stop crying while she dressed.

'You alright?' he asked.

'I'm alright,' she said as mascara ran down her cheeks.

He put on his clothes and shoes and went back into the bathroom and shut the door. When he came out Lynette was putting on her pants. He sat at the desk, brought out his wallet, took cash from it and counted it. He waited until she was fully dressed and then told her to sit on the bed.

'Here's two thousand.' His voice was tired in a way she had never heard. 'And I'm gonna leave another thousand at the front desk tomorrow. I just don't have any more cash on me. The extra two grand is my gift. To help you out, help toward the house. I'm sorry I can't give you more, but I can't. You know why. This is going to be the last time we meet.' He stood up and put on his sport coat. 'Thank you for everything. I've really liked you and I wish you a lot of luck. And as far as investing, just go to one of those places I told you about. They'll help you. And I'd buy the house if you can. This town is getting crazy and if you can get in, get in.' He put the money on the desk and left the room.

Lynette used the toilet and washed her face but still couldn't stop crying. She took the room key, and the shampoo and soap from the bathroom, and put them in her purse, then found his car key behind the desk and left. The room was on the sixth floor and she took the stairs down. In the lobby she saw a woman in a business suit come in the main entrance; in the Driftwood Room there were two couples at a back table. The man was gone.

She walked down Morrison Street and two blocks away she saw him standing in front of his car talking on the phone. Behind a pickup truck she sank down and waited. He hung up and walked back to the hotel.

The car was a black Mercedes S-Class 450. She unlocked it and got in. She took I-405 north, leaving downtown and driving north along the industrial section on Highway 30. When she came to the St Johns Bridge she went across it, then parked the car on a darkened street near the closed-down Tulip Pastry Shop and got out.

7

In front of a bar called Slim's, Lynette called a Radio Cab and waited. The driver took her back across the river to the Hotel deLuxe, where she got her car and drove it to the West Hills where the old mansions of the city were. She parked at the edge of a cul-de-sac and took a heavy drink from a pint of Jägermeister she kept in the glovebox, fixed her make-up and got out. She walked to a 1920s two-storey brick mansion, rang the doorbell and waited.

The man who opened the door was small, thin and dressed in a tight black T-shirt, black jeans and white tennis shoes. His clothes and the shoes looked new. His hair was brown, shaved on the sides and cut short on top. On his face was the same four-day-old beard he always wore. He looked behind her to the driveway and yard and said in a voice that was effeminate and upset, 'What are you doing here?'

'I should have texted first,' said Lynette. 'I'm sorry. I just needed to talk to you. I'm kind of in a bind.'

'Well, it's not a good time,' he said. 'I have people over.'

His driveway was empty and there were no cars on the street alongside his house. She could hear no noise coming from inside and most of the lights were off.

'Come on, let me in. It's freezing out here.'

The man didn't move.

'Then I just need my money.'

'What money?'

'You didn't pay me last time.'

'I didn't?'

'No,' she said.

'I think I did.'

'I keep track of these things. You told me you forgot to go to the bank. You had just flown in from San Jose. You stopped and had dinner at Clyde Common.'

He looked at her. 'I'm pretty sure I paid you that night.'

'Come on,' said Lynette. 'I'm freezing my ass off and my feet are numb. You owe me, you know you do. So let me in or just pay me and I'll leave.'

'You have a lot of nerve.'

'Come on, don't be like that.'

'Be like what?'

'You know.'

'I don't like you just stopping by,' he said. 'That was never the deal.'

'You said that already. I won't do it again. I don't like being here either. Come on, just pay me so I can leave.'

'What, are you a drug addict now?'

'Jesus, no,' she said. 'I just need the money. So give me what you owe me and I'll get out of here.'

He closed the door and locked it. She waited five minutes and when he opened it again he was wearing a down coat. He handed her an envelope. Inside was eight hundred dollars.

'It's two hundred short.'

'That's all I have.'

'I'll take a check for the last two.'

'I don't use checks.'

'You can PayPal me, you have my email.'

'Just take the eight hundred. You're lucky to get that.'

'Lucky? You owe me.'

'That's what you say but I know I paid you for that night. You're just trying to hustle me.'

'Hustle you?' she said. 'Why would I do that? I've never done that before. I just want what I'm owed.'

'Well, I gave you what you're owed. Now I want you to leave. I'll call you when I want you but don't ever come here like this again.'

'I'd rather kill myself than come here again,' she said in a voice that was weak and shook slightly. 'I've never liked you, not even for a moment. You've always just been an entitled rich asshole to me. A pervert too, and I want you to know that I always had to have a couple drinks to knock on your door and I had to be half-shitfaced to take off my clothes in front of you. And there wasn't a single time I didn't feel horrible and creepy afterward. Not once.'

The twenty-eight-year-old IT executive couldn't look at her but didn't move from the doorway as she walked toward her car.

★

It was almost three years since three separate loan officers had limited her mother to a two-hundred-thousand-dollar home loan. In desperation Lynette had promised she would get the rest, eighty thousand dollars. 'Don't worry. I have almost three years to figure out how, and I will,' she'd told her mother. Within a week of that promise she had the second job at The Dutchman and took every extra shift she could get, both there and at the bakery. She quit eating out and never bought herself anything that wasn't needed. She had two years and nine months until their landlord had said he would sell their house, so she worked and worked and worked. But after ten months she realized there was no way she would come up with that kind of money.

When she confessed her situation to Gloria, a coworker at The Dutchman, Gloria told her she knew how Lynette could make that money and more. Gloria was a part-time escort and told her about it over drinks after work. Lynette went home from their meeting half-drunk and spent the rest of the night in bed, sobbing. A week later Gloria introduced her to the bald pudgy man.

She met the IT man at the RingSide Steakhouse: Lynette, him, his coworker and Gloria. After dinner Lynette and the IT man moved to the bar, sat by themselves and awkwardly came up with an agreement that Gloria had planned out for her. He drove her back to his house and it began.

He was timid the first three times they were together but after that he began sending her text messages telling her what he wanted to do and how he wanted her to look. In person they seldom spoke and never discussed his texts or what he wanted. During sex, if he came too quickly, he'd sulk and oftentimes become cruel. If he felt like he had done a good job then he would be nicer to her. He would lounge around longer before dressing. He'd make jokes and flirt.

As time passed his texts became more demanding and aggressive but she never once complained. She only thought about the money and complied with how he wanted her to look and what he wanted her to do. On Gloria's advice, with each new thing he asked, she charged more. But it began to drag on her and she dreaded the nights with him. After a while she had to be drunk just to walk up his drive, and always, no matter what, as she drove home after a night with him she broke down crying.

A personal trainer came to the man's house four days a week. He hired a woman to pick out and buy his clothes. He bleached his teeth and had pedicures and manicures. He waxed his back and his pubic and leg hair. To be with him she had to do the same. His personal bathroom was covered completely in mirrors, even the ceiling, and there were times they had sex in it just so he could watch himself.

He'd paid for the house in the West Hills with cash and had it completely remodelled before he moved in. An interior designer oversaw the project and decorated it. She picked the furniture, the photos, the dishes, the appliances, even the bath towels and sheets. The house had five bedrooms, an oak-panelled study, a gym and recreation room in the basement, and four full bathrooms. The floors were high-gloss oak. The walls were flat white and each held a single abstract black-and-white photo. All the furniture was black and uncomfortable except in the basement, where he had a soft leather couch and an entertainment centre with the largest TV she had ever seen. The kitchen had a professional-grade range even though he didn't cook, a stainless-steel refrigerator-freezer filled with juices, beer, condiments, sparkling water and pre-made meals a woman cooked for him each week. Another woman did his laundry and his grocery shopping and cleaned the house.

Lynette came every two weeks and he paid her a thousand dollars each time; she had seen him twenty-six times. Eight of those nights, when he'd asked something more of her, he had given her a tip, sometimes an extra thousand dollars. The only problem that arose was that he wouldn't pay her until the end of the night. By then he didn't want her any more. He would say he didn't have the money or that it was too much or that she wasn't worth it. By their eleventh time together, and all times after, Lynette had to demand to get paid. It became a struggle between them and eventually, nearly always, by the end of the night she was left to beg.

8

On the third try the car started, and she left the West Hills, drove across the Ross Island Bridge and headed south on Milwaukie. It was ten thirty and when the only Dairy Queen open until eleven finally appeared, she parked and went inside. The place was empty but for a high-school-aged girl with glasses and brown hair standing behind the register.

'I'm sorry but we're closing in twenty minutes,' the girl said. 'The grill's just been shut off.'

'That's okay,' said Lynette. 'I just want a Peanut Buster Parfait for here and one to go. And do you have coffee?'

'Yeah, but it's been sitting forever. You can have it for free if you want.'

Lynette nodded, handed her ten dollars and the girl rang her up.

In the corner of the empty Dairy Queen she sat in a booth. A heat vent on the ceiling blew down warm air and she took off her coat and scarf and drank the burned coffee. Tears welled in her eyes and she couldn't stop them. In one day, years of her planning and struggle and sacrifice had come to mean nothing. There would be no house; she wouldn't be able to provide that for Kenny or her mother. She had failed.

Her plan had been to hire her father's crew for a day. If she did the prep work they could have painted the entire main floor in that amount of time. There was also a baker at 9th Street who was an artist and Lynette had been going to hire him to paint the Trail Blazers and Winterhawks logos on the walls in Kenny's room. A licensed electrician named Roy Oldham, a regular at The Dutchman, had said he would give her a full day of work for a month of free drinks. She had plans for the bathroom, the kitchen and the basement, all written in a notebook she'd look at when she couldn't sleep or was on break at work.

She began eating the Peanut Buster Parfait and looked at the clock on the wall. Seventeen more minutes until they closed. A couple in their twenties entered and went to the counter. The man whispered in the woman's ear, she ordered for both of them and the same girl rang them up. The couple stepped back and the woman took off the man's baseball cap and shook the rain from it. She ran her hands through his hair and put it back on. They each had a Chocolate Dipped Cone and sat at a table across from each other.

Three more people came in after that, two tall teenage girls and a man wearing a canvas coat and a hat that read *Gifford Construction*. The girls looked like sisters and the man their father. They sat in the booth across from Lynette. The girls wore matching sweats that had a large yellow *M* and a mustang on them. Milwaukie High School. They had come from a swim meet in Eugene and both girls complained that they hadn't made the finals. Their father listened and when they finished he told them how great he thought they'd done.

'But you always say that,' one of the girls said while eating a Blizzard. 'And tonight we both sucked.'

'Not making the finals doesn't really mean you're bad,' the father said, and at that the two girls began laughing.

Lynette finished the Peanut Buster Parfait, closed her eyes and thought about swimming. When she was a freshman in high school she'd made friends with a girl who had just moved to Portland from Seattle. The girl said her parents had a cabin on Hood Canal in Washington. 'All we do all summer is swim and lie on a raft and eat. You should come up.'

The girl had told her this only in passing, just one day while they ate lunch together, but that night Lynette hadn't been able to sleep because she wanted to go with the girl to Hood Canal, she wanted to swim all day and lie on a raft, but she didn't know how to swim. She had never learned how. For nearly a month she worried about it and then one Saturday she took Kenny to the Northeast Community Center and told a woman there that neither she nor Kenny could swim and she was wondering if they could take lessons together. The woman signed them up for the adult/teens class every Wednesday at 7 p.m. and charged her for only one person, sixty dollars.

Lynette had only twenty dollars but that evening, when they got home, she put the nine CDs she owned in a pile to sell and when her mother and Randy went to sleep she went through her mother's purse and took thirty dollars. Her mother never mentioned the missing money and every Wednesday after that Lynette took Kenny to swim class. Her mother must have known Lynette couldn't swim either but she said nothing about it and let them go.

From the beginning, however, Lynette was terrified of the water and so embarrassed and scared that she could barely walk out to the pool. She and Kenny would put on their swimsuits in the handicapped bathroom but always, just before they left, she'd say to Kenny, 'I can't do it.' She would sit on the toilet seat and sob and Kenny, who was excited to get in the water, would try to pull her outside. 'Please don't make me,' she'd say. 'Please don't.' But her brother wouldn't stop pulling on her arm until she opened the bathroom door and they went outside to the showers to rinse off before class. They had learned to swim together and she had learned to like it, and when the classes ended, they even kept going for a while.

★

'I'm sorry but we're closing now,' a voice said. 'I let you stay an extra ten minutes.'

Lynette opened her eyes to see that the family and the young couple had left. The Dairy Queen was again empty and the counter girl was standing by Lynette smiling.

'Here's the extra Peanut Buster Parfait you ordered. I kept it in the freezer for you.' She set down the ice cream in a white paper bag. Lynette looked at her and tried to speak but couldn't.

9

The car started on the first try and she headed north to Belmont Street and parked. There was a hard rain falling. She ran past a half-built condominium complex and stopped at the entrance of a new five-storey apartment building. She entered a code, the main door opened and she took an elevator to the fifth floor and knocked on apartment fifty-one. A minute passed and then a woman in a black silk bathrobe answered.

'What are you doing here?' the woman exclaimed. 'I'm in a hurry. I gotta leave in a few minutes.'

'I'll only be a minute,' said Lynette. The woman shook her head but stepped back and Lynette walked into a large open room that overlooked Belmont Street.

A white shag rug covered most of the floor and on it sat a brown leather couch, a long glass coffee table and two matching brown leather chairs. A five-foot-wide TV hung from the wall.

'I know I should have called, but at least I brought you ice cream,' said Lynette, and followed the woman into the kitchen.

'What kind?'

'A Peanut Buster Parfait.' Lynette took off her scarf and coat and set them on a stool.

'Is that Dairy Queen?'

'Yeah.'

The woman went to the fridge, took an open bottle of champagne from it, poured a glass and headed for the bathroom. Lynette followed behind her.

'I can't eat shit like that any more and not gain weight. It all goes to my stomach and nowhere else. Sorry if I was a bitch. I'm just stressed and I didn't know you were coming over. You have to call first. Anyway, I have to get out of here in fifteen minutes. Terry got mad at me last week for being late. Old people hate when you're late and it was the first time he ever got mad at me. He looks like my grandmother when he gets upset.'

Lynette sat on the edge of the bathtub. 'Jesus, you keep this place warm. It's like heaven.'

The woman looked at Lynette in the reflection of the mirror. 'What happened to you? You look like shit.'

Lynette shrugged and just watched as she put on her make-up.

Gloria Milligan was the most beautiful woman Lynette had ever met. Thin and tall with black hair and light-blue eyes. She had a seemingly natural elegance to her, but Lynette knew she had worked hard at it. Gloria was neither elegant nor educated. When drinking or in a bad mood she could slip up and show her true self: a mean, often crude, drunk who looked out only for herself, who could be vindictive and cruel. The old man she was with had witnessed none of it. He thought she'd grown up in Portland and had gone to college at UC Berkeley. That she was an only child whose parents had died in a car wreck when she was in high school. A girl born to money but who now had none of it.

Lynette knew the truth. Gloria had grown up in the logging town of Clatskanie. When drunk, she could disappear into tirades about her past life in a single-wide trailer with her mother and father, a brother and two sisters. Her father, a one-time truck driver, was partially paralyzed from a stroke and the family had been forced to live on her mother's waitressing job, food stamps, a disability check, and a two-hundred-dollar monthly stipend from her mother's parents.

It was Gloria's looks that had both saved and ruined her. By age fifteen she was constantly sought after. Her brother's friends came by unannounced, her two sisters' boyfriends flirted with her, her dad's friends hit on her, her coworkers at the pizza parlour would punch her in before she showed up, and two of her high-school teachers gave her passing grades when she didn't deserve them.

It had been seven years since she'd had contact with her family and now, at twenty-eight, she had a cocaine habit and failing vision. She couldn't drive at night and had difficulty reading signs even in daylight. She told nobody but had drunkenly confessed it to Lynette one night: 'I have macular degeneration. I'll be blind in five years,' she'd cried. 'Completely blind.'

Gloria moved her face in front of the mirror and did her eyes.

'I just got back from Newport Beach,' she said. 'Did I tell you?'

'I don't think so. Where is that?'

'In Southern California. You never go anywhere, do you?'

'No, not really,' said Lynette.

'I love it there. Terry had business in Corona del Mar. I flew down a couple days after him but he didn't even put me in first class. He used to always put me in first class. I hope he just made a mistake but I don't think so. He never makes mistakes like that. Anyway, we got two rooms at the Hyatt. The weather was perfect. I saw him for a total of eight hours in three days. That's the kind of trip I like.'

'What did you do?'

'Sat by the pool, had a massage, went shopping. I bought a Chloé Marcie bag, a couple dresses and some lingerie. It was a three-thousand-dollar bill, but he didn't bat an eye. So that's a good sign. But the hotel was lame. Terry says he'll never stay at another Hyatt. He doesn't like their beds. I don't like them either and if you ask me, the whole place is tacky.'

Lynette laughed.

'What's so funny?'

'You grew up sleeping on a couch and now you're complaining about a fancy bed at the Hyatt.'

Gloria glared at her in the reflection of the mirror. 'I've told you a million times not to bring up my past, but you never fucking listen. So watch it or I won't want to be around you any more.'

'I'm sorry,' said Lynette. 'It just slipped out.'

Gloria finished her eyes and began putting on lipstick. 'Back then just makes me think about my dad eating Safeway fried chicken and drinking grape soda and watching TV all day. We had one bathroom for six people, imagine that. My mom always smelled like bar food and she'd get so depressed she'd just sit at the kitchen table and drink beer on ice. Thinking about it just for a second gets me in a bad mood and you somehow always make me think about it.'

'I know. I'm sorry,' said Lynette. 'I didn't mean to, I really didn't.'

Gloria put the cap back on the lipstick. 'Does my make-up look alright?'

Lynette went to her and looked at her face. 'You did good.'

Gloria stepped back and opened her robe to show black lingerie. 'Look at these, Simone Pérèle. It's like wearing happiness.'

'Where are you going so late?'

'Terry got a room at the Sentinel, downtown. He was in Lake Oswego seeing his brother and their dinner ran late so he decided he didn't want to drive back to Seattle tonight. I had other plans but I had to cancel them when he called. I've been sitting around waiting for his text and finally he sent it. We're gonna have a drink in the bar and then I'm spending the night. But I'm scared he's getting tired of me. He didn't want to have sex the last two times we were together. But he told me in California that he loved me. That he was in love with me. He'd had a couple drinks but he's never said that before. So I don't know what to think. If he gets me a condo he can have me forever. I mean it too. I don't care. It's not that much work. I like him enough. But he always shuts down when I bring it up. At least I'm getting money off him – he pays the rent here and usually gives me whatever I ask for. But I want a condo.'

Gloria went to the bedroom and Lynette followed her. It was a large room with the same white shag carpet, a white dresser and white bedside table, and a king-sized bed with a white down comforter. A closet ran the length of the room where dresses and blouses and coats hung. On the floor sat rows of shoes and in the far corner of the closet, half-hidden under a blanket, Lynette saw a safe.

Gloria took off her robe and put on a black cocktail dress. 'So what happened to you?'

'Nothing I really want to talk about right now,' said Lynette, and sat on the edge of the bed. 'And I know you're in a hurry, but I was hoping I could get back the money I loaned you.'

'The money?'

'The eight thousand dollars I gave you.'

Gloria looked at her.

'For the DUI? You told me you were gonna give me the money back within a week, no problem. But it's been seven months.'

'When do you need it?' said Gloria, and zipped up the back of her dress. She dropped to her knees and began looking for the shoes she wanted but had trouble seeing them in the dim light of the room. One by one, she picked a shoe and brought it just inches from her eyes.

'Can you give it to me tonight?'

'Tonight?' cried Gloria. She found a pair of black high heels and put them on.

'I know it's not much notice,' said Lynette, and fell back on the bed. 'I guess things have just kind of fallen apart for me.'

Gloria turned on the overhead lights and stood in front of a mirror on the back wall. 'I wish I could give it to you but I don't have it. I'm broke.'

'You're broke?'

'Flat broke.'

Lynette sat back up. 'I thought Terry gave you a thousand a week spending money.'

'Sometimes he does. Not all the time. Not lately.'

'What about those two other guys you're seeing?'

'What the fuck?' said Gloria, and again glared at her through the reflection in the mirror. 'I'm not seeing them any more. And don't tell anyone I am. I don't like how you always bring up stuff I don't want you to bring up.'

'Sorry,' said Lynette. 'I just know last week you said you were seeing two other guys, that's all. Now you're not?'

'What are you, the fucking police? I'll get you the money. I just don't have it and now you're making me late. And if Terry breaks up with me you'll never get it.'

'Alright,' said Lynette. 'Like I said, I'm just in a fix and I'm having a hard time and I might need to find a new place to live. So I have to ask. When do you think you could get it?'

'Honestly, I don't know. You can't just throw things like this at me when I'm trying not to be late.'

'You don't have even a rough idea?'

'If I don't have it, I don't have it. You should have called and warned me about all this.' Gloria left the room and Lynette got off the bed and followed her to the kitchen. 'An Uber is going to be here in five minutes.' She poured more champagne into her glass. 'Look, I didn't mean to get pissed off. I got a lot going on too. I'll get Terry to give me some money tonight. I could probably get you five hundred.'

Lynette nodded. She sat on a stool at the kitchen counter. 'Is it alright if I stay here?' she asked. 'I just can't go home right now.'

'Sure,' said Gloria, putting on a coat and grabbing her purse. 'I won't be here until tomorrow anyway.'

'I really appreciate it. And do you have an extra key? I'm going to get some food and then come back.'

Gloria looked in a kitchen drawer, found a spare key and gave it to her. 'I have to get downstairs. Can you check my face one more time?'

Lynette looked over her make-up, told her it was fine and Gloria left. Lynette waited five minutes then went back to the bedroom and to the small safe in the corner of the closet. She gave it a shove and it moved. It wasn't bolted down but it was too heavy to pick up. She sat on the bed, tried to think, and then took a half-dozen pictures of it and left.

10

There was an unmarked door in the back of The Dutch-man's restaurant that led to the kitchen. Lynette knocked on it until the night cleaner opened it.

'What do you want?' said the tall man standing in the doorway.

'I don't know if you recognize me, but I'm Lynette. I've worked in the bar the last few years. We've met a couple times.'

'I know who you are,' he said. 'Why don't you go in through the bar entrance?'

'Because I want to talk to you.'

'Me?' he said. 'Why would you want to talk to me?'

'Your name is Cody, right?'

He nodded. 'Why do you want to know?'

'I just wanted to make sure I was talking to the right guy. Will you let me in? It's freezing out here and I'm getting soaked.'

He stepped back and let her in.

Cody was six feet three inches tall and weighed less than a hundred and forty pounds. He was so thin and gaunt he looked ill. He had a straggly beard and his hair was curly, brown and long. There were dime-sized holes in his earlobes where he'd once had piercings. His nose was narrow and long and drooped at the end, and his arms were bony and covered in new, brightly coloured tattoos.

He moved back into the kitchen and Lynette shut the door behind her. Fluorescent lights shone down from the ceiling and a radio was playing. The kitchen smelled of bacon grease, bleach and cigarette smoke.

Cody leaned against the prep counter. 'What do you want with me?'

'I heard you've been in prison.'

'What's it to you?' he said, and took a pack of cigarettes from his pants pocket and lit one.

'You're not supposed to smoke in here.'

'Why do you care?'

Lynette shrugged. 'Sorry, you're right. I have something to ask but I need to know a few things first. What were you in prison for?'

'Burglary.'

'That's what I heard,' said Lynette. 'What did you steal?'

'Why do you want to know?'

'I just want to know.'

A half-full pot of coffee sat on a warmer. He went to it and poured some into a metal travel mug, then added five packets of sugar and stirred it with a fork. 'I've stole a lot of things, but right now I just want to get out of here and you're getting in the way of that. So what do you want?'

'I need help doing something illegal and I didn't know who else to ask. Shirley told me you'd been in prison so I thought of you and I knew you were working tonight.'

He shook his head. 'The last thing I'm gonna do is anything illegal. Anyway, I don't even know you.'

'Are you sure?'

'I'm sure.'

'Okay, I understand,' said Lynette. 'I don't know that much about things like this and it's probably a bad idea so I'll just leave you alone. But please don't tell anyone I came to you.'

She headed for the door and was nearly to it when Cody said, 'I ain't gonna do whatever you're thinking, but what is it?'

She went back to him, stood less than a foot away and whispered, 'There's a safe I want but I'm not strong enough to carry it out and I don't know how to open it.'

'You want me to help you steal a safe?' His breath smelled of coffee and cigarettes and teeth that he didn't brush. He picked up a mop leaned against the sink, put it in the bucket and rinsed it out. He took a drink of coffee and began mopping. 'No way.'

'We could take it somewhere and you could figure out how to open it. I can move it around so it's not bolted down and it's not that heavy either. I'm just not strong enough to carry it alone.'

He kept mopping.

'I have the key to the place and the owner is gone all night.'

Cody stopped and looked at her. 'Where is it?'

'An apartment ten minutes from here.'

'What kind of safe?'

'It's a SentrySafe. I don't know what that means but that's what it says on it. When I looked it up it said you could buy them at Home Depot.' She took the phone from her purse and showed him three pictures of it.

'What's inside it?'

'I'm not sure, that's the problem. But I'll give you a third of what's mine if there's money in it. Someone owes me and I don't think they'll ever pay me back.'

'How much do they owe you?'

'Eight thousand dollars.'

'Shit,' he said. 'Where did you get eight grand?'

She shrugged.

He scratched his beard with his left hand, then took a phone from his back pocket and punched in numbers. When he was done he looked at her. 'Thirty per cent of eight grand is twenty-four hundred. That's a lot of money. The problem is, everybody's got cameras now. They'll know we took it.'

'She doesn't have cameras inside her place. I don't know about the building. But she won't report it anyway. She won't call the cops if I just take what's mine. I know she won't. And if you can't open it there, we'll have to bring the safe and the stuff in it back when we're done.'

'Shit, I won't be able to open it at her place. I ain't a safe-cracker. If it's not bolted down like you say, we'll just take it. We'll borrow the hand truck here. You have a car?'

Lynette nodded.

'And you have to do this tonight?'

'I'll lose my nerve if it's not tonight. Plus I have the key to the apartment and I've never had the key before.'

Cody took a drag on his cigarette and looked at her. 'Well, I'm not going back to a place I just robbed. And we'll probably have to destroy the safe to get it open . . . I know a mechanic who has a lot of tools. I haven't talked to him in a while but I bet he could do it. I just don't know if he'd want to. Either way, the safe will be fucked. When we get it open you can take the stuff inside back if you want. But I'm not gonna get involved in that. Once I leave there I'm never going back.'

'Fair enough,' she said.

'And you're serious?' he said.

'Yeah. Will you do it?'

'Maybe. Let me call the mechanic and see if he's around.'

Cody leaned the mop against a prep table, walked out to the restaurant and made the call. He came back five minutes later.

'The mechanic says he'll do it. He's not that far from here, around 82nd and Johnson Creek. He's an old-time speed freak but he's got a shop and a ton of tools. He said he'll open it for five hundred. You have five hundred in cash?'

Lynette nodded.

'And if there's nothing in there, I want five hundred too.'

'Alright,' she said.

'That's a thousand cash total. You have that?'

'Yes.'

'On you?'

Again she nodded.

He rubbed his face with his hands so hard she thought he might be on something and then he blew his nose into a rag that was sitting on the edge of the sink. 'I'm gonna help you 'cause I've been riding the bus for a year and I'm tired of it. It takes me an hour and fifteen minutes just to get here. I need to get a car.'

'Can you go now?'

'I have to finish cleaning first. I can't lose this job. I have to keep this job.'

'I can help you if you want. We can get out of here sooner then.'

'Really?'

'Sure.'

'Alright, then,' he said. 'You finish mopping the kitchen and I'll clean both sinks and toilets, then you mop the bathroom floors while I vacuum the restaurant.'

Lynette took the mop from him. The bucket was full of cold brown and greasy water. She went to the utility sink, emptied the bucket, cleaned it out and filled it with hot water and soap, and began mopping the kitchen floor.

★

They put the hand truck in the back of the Nissan and Cody sat crammed in the passenger seat, his knees hitting the glovebox, his hair touching the roof. His coat was a faded black hoodie. The rain continued to fall and the clock on the dashboard said 12.35 a.m.

'You should have the mechanic look at your car after he opens the safe,' said Cody. 'It's missing. Can you hear it making that tapping sound?'

'I think so.'

'Does it have less power than it usually does?'

'Yeah,' she said.

'And trouble starting?'

She nodded.

'It's not running on all four cylinders.'

'Is that bad?'

'The engine is probably fucked. You mind if I smoke?'

'Go ahead.'

Cody took a pack of Marlboro Reds from his hoodie pocket and lit one. He wiped the window glass with his sleeve. 'It's cold as fuck in here. Doesn't your heater work?'

'When I turn the heat on it smells like antifreeze. It makes you sick to your stomach if you leave it on.'

He cracked the window and blew the cigarette smoke out.

'It's your heater core. It's probably busted.'

'What's that?'

'It's a little radiator that heats your car. It's probably leaking.'

'Is that expensive to fix?'

'On most cars you have to pull out the dash to do it. The part ain't expensive but putting it in is.'

Lynette sighed and leaned against the driver's-side door.

'So you freeze your ass off all the time?'

'Yeah,' she said. 'But I wear long underwear from November on. It's not so bad. Can I ask you something?'

'Maybe?'

'What did you steal to get thrown in prison?'

'Why do you want to know?'

She shrugged. 'I figured since we're doing this I should know.'

Cody let out a plume of smoke and said, 'My girlfriend at the time worked at an old folks' home in Sherwood. She planned it and me and this guy robbed it.'

'You guys robbed an old folks' home?'

'Yeah.'

'And you got caught?'

'They set me up and I didn't see it coming.' He again wiped the passenger-side window glass with his arm. 'The other guy was a friend of hers. I only met him a couple times and he seemed alright. We wore masks and locked this old night nurse in a closet. This was before everybody had cameras everywhere. We took all the meds. That was the main thing. But since we were there, we also took the TVs and stole the old people's personal shit. We had a van and his car. The car had all the personal shit from the residents, the meds, and smaller things. The van had the bigger stuff, like the TVs and anything we couldn't fit in the car. It went off no problem and we left. I drove the van, he drove the car. The plan was to keep the TVs in a barn until he could sell them. We had maybe thirty of them. He said he knew how to get rid of stuff like that where we'd actually make some money. Outside of St Helens his grandmother had a place with an old dairy barn. The plan was, he was gonna drop the stuff from the car at my girlfriend's place and then meet me at the barn and we'd unload the van. I got out there and waited for a while, then just started unloading the shit when a cop car pulled up and that was it. The police had been tipped off and they took me in. After a while I told them about the guy I did the job with. They tracked him down and he told the cops he didn't know anything about the robbery. He said he had no idea why I would put stuff into his grandmother's barn or how I even knew where his grandmother lived. He said he barely knew me, just heard

76

about me from his girlfriend. He said his girlfriend used to go out with me and that I was jealous and had spent a lot of time in juvie. And then I figured it out. He was seeing my girlfriend. That's who he was talking about. They were engaged. They had wedding plans. I had no fucking idea. He told the cops they were together the night of the robbery and she verified it. A friend of hers who I didn't know also verified it. I told the cops he had all the drugs and the residents' personal shit but nothing came of that. I don't know if they even checked. All I know is I spent four years in Pendleton. I could have gone away for ten, but my mom got me a good lawyer.'

'What happened to your girlfriend?'

'Nothing. She told the police we'd broken up 'cause I was jealous and could be violent. She said she thought that's why I did it. To get back at her for breaking up with me. She showed them emails. I mean, she even got on my laptop and sent herself emails from my account. She pretended to be me. The emails were rants, mean as shit, saying I was gonna ruin her life. It looked bad. I told the cops that I hated writing emails. I hate typing. I just text. I couldn't remember the last time I emailed somebody. So I never checked it and I sure as fuck didn't check my sent file. But, of course, the cops didn't believe that. The people that ran the old folks' home were on her side too. She didn't get fired or even reprimanded and she was the one who told me what to steal out of which rooms. She used to do inventory of the old fuckers' stuff. She hated those old people. She really did . . . One day I'll get back at her. I mean, what type of person would do that?'

'But you robbed old sick people.'

'I guess,' he said. 'But most of them couldn't even remember their names. What are they gonna do with a watch or a phone or a gold ring? Plus, all that shit's insured. Everything in the van I took was insured so why should anyone really care?'

They came to a stop light and Lynette wiped the inside of the window glass with a rag. 'We got robbed once when I was fifteen,' she said. 'It was between Christmas and New Year's so I was home on break. My mom was at work. I was in the basement, asleep. I woke up to my brother screaming. He's developmentally disabled. He had headphones on in his room and was watching a movie. Two guys broke in, they climbed in through a window, and stole our TV and a portable stereo and they ransacked the living room and kitchen. You'd think I would have heard but I didn't. They went through my mom's room. Everything in her dresser drawers they threw on the ground. Then they went into the back bedroom and found my brother in bed watching TV. My brother was so scared he started screaming. He got out of bed and tried to run but they threw him against the wall. I'd woken up by then and ran up the stairs. I didn't know what was going on, I just knew something was wrong. I could hear all the different footsteps on the floor and as I got to the kitchen I could hear men's voices. I thought I was gonna have a heart attack. Nothing like that had ever happened in our house. Jesus, I was scared. And then I saw them, they were bums, and they were in our living room grabbing all the stuff they could carry. They were both on bikes with those little yellow trailers behind them.

The kind people put kids in. They put our things in there. I just watched them do it. I didn't do anything. I was too scared to try and stop them. None of the stuff we had was any good – I mean, they couldn't have made much off it. But it ruined us for a long time and was really hard on my brother. He couldn't be alone for months after but the truth is I didn't like being alone in the house either. We were both scared. Even when summer came, when it was hot out, we kept the windows shut and locked until our mom came home. We got an alarm system even though we had no money. My mom had to call up my aunt and ask her for a loan so we could get it. But we didn't know what else to do. Me and my brother were alone at home most of the time and my mom was too scared about that without an alarm. I remember when the cops came to talk to us about the men – they showed us the window screen the guys cut and how they jimmied the window open. It was awful . . . My brother was so scared. He doesn't like men anyway, and after that it was twice as bad. For a while he'd get really agitated at any man we saw that looked like them. Those fuckers made our life really hard and probably didn't get more than fifty bucks for all of it combined.'

'You have renters' insurance?'

'No.'

'You should have had it. Then you would have gotten new shit. Those guys would have done you a favour then.'

'That's not the point.'

'And you should have had your windows locked better.'

'Fuck you,' said Lynette. 'Those guys made it so my brother couldn't be alone for months. He had to sleep next to me and he wakes up every hour. My mom had to borrow money to get us a new TV. We were that broke.'

'Why are you on my ass? I didn't do it.'

'Maybe,' she said. 'I've just never liked thieves.'

'Well, I only rob people where there's shit I could actually sell and make money. But like I said, I don't do that any more. Anyway, don't fuck with me. I'm helping you.'

11

From the time he got out of the car on Belmont Street, Cody kept his hoodie up and his eyes on the ground. In the elevator he put on a pair of latex kitchen gloves and followed Lynette into Gloria's apartment. He stood hunched over like an old man and waited with the hand truck in the living room. Lynette walked through the apartment and called out Gloria's name. She checked each room, then came back to Cody and nervously whispered, 'There's no one here.' They didn't speak again and she led him to the bedroom. They moved the safe out of the closet, set it on the hand truck and wheeled it to the main room. Cody took two towels from the bathroom and covered the safe with them and they left. They'd been inside Gloria's apartment less than three minutes.

There was no one in the hall or in the elevator when they went down and Cody never once looked up or spoke. Outside it was still raining and no one was on the street. They wheeled the safe to her car, a block away, and not even a single car passed. Together they lifted it into the trunk but the safe was too big for the lid to shut so Cody found a pair of jumper cables and tied the lid down. They put the hand truck in the back seat and got in the car.

Lynette's hands were shaking as she put the key into the ignition, and the car started on the third try. Cody took off his gloves, put them in his hoodie pocket, and they kept silent until she turned south on 82nd Avenue.

'I feel like I'm gonna throw up,' she said.

'But it's a good rush, isn't?' said Cody, and lit a cigarette.

'Maybe. I don't know. I feel horrible too.'

'It's too late to feel horrible,' he said, and blew out a line of smoke through the crack in the window. 'Now we just gotta hope there's something in the safe.'

Lynette wiped the inside of the windshield with the rag. 'I've never really stolen anything before.'

'Really?'

'Yeah.'

'I used to like it. Especially before I was eighteen and it was no big deal to get busted. But I'm over it now.'

They fell silent again and then Cody told her to turn down a side street and then another, and finally he threw his cigarette out the window and told her to stop. He pointed to a two-storey Craftsman house at the end of a road.

'There's a gravel drive to the left of that fucked-up-looking house,' he said. 'The house is his but I've never been in it. He spends all his time in the pole barn behind it.'

'How do you know him?'

'In high school I lived a couple blocks away from here. For a while he worked on my mom's car but my mom got scared of him. He also sold weed and he'd buy kids in the neighbourhood beer if we paid him enough. Ten bucks a twelve-pack plus the cost of the beer.' He coughed again and rolled down the window and spat. 'He's a weird fucker so let's talk to him before we get the safe out of the trunk, okay?'

'Okay. But how's he weird?'

'He's just a weirdo so we have to see what kind of mood he's in and how long he's been up. Like I said, I haven't seen him in a while but if he's in the wrong sorta mood we'll just leave and figure out somewhere else to take it. If he seems alright then we'll bring it in.'

'I'm starting to get scared,' she said, and looked over at him. 'Are you sure we should go there?'

'No, not really,' he said, 'but I can't think of anyone else and I can't take it back to my place. I'm on parole.'

'You're on parole?' said Lynette with growing alarm.

He nodded. 'Can we take it to your house?'

'No.'

'You could always leave it in your trunk and figure out some other way later. Give me my five hundred and drop me back at The Dutchman. It's your call.'

'But tomorrow my friend will know.' Lynette wiped the windshield with the rag and looked out.

'Fuck it, I want to see what's in there,' Cody finally said. 'Let's just drive down there and we'll see how it goes.'

★

The derelict house was white in colour but hadn't been painted in decades and was half-covered in blackberry bushes. Steel bars covered the windows, even on the second floor, and cardboard was taped to the inside of the window glass, keeping out any light. Lynette drove past it and came to a large gravel turnaround and a weathered lime-green shop. The car's headlights shone on a dented roll-up door that read, in faded red paint, *Johnson Creek Auto Repair*.

When she turned off the ignition they were in complete darkness and the only sound came from rain beating down on the hood of the car. Cody used the flashlight on his phone so they could see their way as they headed down the side of the building. A ten-foot chain-link fence ran along the left edge of the property. Dogs barked frantically from the house next door. Lynette's feet were numb and she was beginning to have trouble breathing.

They came to a single small light bulb that hung over a metal door and Cody knocked. It took two minutes before a thin man with dyed blonde hair opened it. He smelled of gasoline and wore stained grey mechanic's coveralls. He didn't speak, just waved them in. His right leg buckled with each step as he backed up. He shut the door behind them and they walked into the light of the shop to see that more than half of his face was covered in psoriasis. Red bursting blisters ran from the back of his neck around his left ear and completely engulfed his left eye and forehead. He was young, in his twenties, but his teeth had gone bad and his eyes looked pushed into his head like he was an old man.

Sets of fluorescent lights hung over a ten-foot-long workbench where a large overweight man, in the same type of grey mechanic's coveralls, stood next to a wood stove. The walls were lined with shelves of used car parts and in the back of the shop a red pickup truck sat on a lift six feet off the ground.

'Hey, Kansas,' Cody said. 'Long time no see. How you been?'

'Why is she here? I didn't say you could bring her,' was the first thing he said. His voice had a high-pitched grate to it, like something in his voice box was broken. His tongue was pierced and there was a large silver stud in the middle of it that he played with when he talked. He had a grey beard and a red bandana covered his head. He walked to a battered refrigerator and took out a can of Hamm's beer while the man with the blonde hair grabbed a spray bottle full of gasoline from the workbench, squirted some into a dust mask and put the mask on his face.

Cody backed up toward the door. 'You didn't say not to so I thought it would be alright. She's the one that knew about the safe. But if it's too much, man, we'll just get out of here.'

'Where is it?' asked Kansas.

'In the trunk of her car,' said Cody.

'What kind is it?'

Lynette stood behind Cody and in a near-whisper said, 'I took some pictures of it. All it says on it is *SentrySafe*.'

'Did you see a model number?'

'No.'

'So it's in your car?'

'Yes.'

'Then let's get it,' he said, and pointed to the door. The man with the blonde hair limped over and opened it. Kansas went out first, followed by Lynette. He smelled of beer, rotten body odour and gasoline. He didn't say anything and they walked in near darkness. When they came to the car he untied the jumper cables and the trunk sprang open. He leaned over and picked up the safe, grunting in short bursts and then beginning to wheeze, but he got it in his arms and stumbled back to the shop. Inside, he dropped it on the concrete floor near the workbench.

'What's in it?' he gasped.

'I don't know,' said Lynette. 'But like Cody told you, I'll give you five hundred dollars for opening it, but whatever's inside is mine.'

'Then give me the five hundred now,' said Kansas. 'I don't want to get involved with anything else. As far as I know, it's your safe and you forgot the combination. Good enough?'

Lynette nodded, took five hundred dollars from her front pants pocket and set it on the workbench. Kansas counted it and put it in his pocket. From the back of the shop he brought out two four-foot-long crowbars and went to work on the safe. He wheezed as he jammed the first crowbar into the edges of the door, trying to bend it. After five minutes he had both crowbars inside the safe and he bent the door until it popped open.

From inside he took out three rubber-banded stacks of one-hundred-dollar bills, a large plastic bag of what looked like cocaine, three diamond rings, two silver dollars in cases, an antique gold necklace, an antique brooch, a manila envelope of papers, and stacks of personal and family photos.

12

Kansas laid it all out on the workbench and Lynette knew, just by seeing the things in the stark bright light, that the man would change his mind. She rushed to the table and began shoving Gloria's things inside her purse but the man with the blonde hair cried out in the voice of a boy, 'She's stealing it!'

Kansas yelled at her to stop but Lynette kept going until everything from the safe was inside her purse.

'I paid you the five hundred I owed you,' she said nervously while backing up. 'That was the deal.'

Kansas moved toward her and pointed at the purse. 'Put the stuff back on the table.'

'But that wasn't what we agreed,' said Lynette. 'You can take the drugs if you want. But I have to give back her personal stuff and the extra money. I just want what's mine. I already paid you for opening it and you're the one who said you didn't want anything else to do with it.'

'Give Cody the drugs,' said Kansas. 'That'll be his cut.'

'His cut?' said Lynette.

'Jesus, man, I don't want them,' said Cody. 'They piss-test me and I'll end up doing it if I take it. I just want my part of the money and half of the jewellery. Let's count it and see how much there is. She says eight grand is hers. I just want my cut of that and I'll take the rings and the silver dollars.'

The blonde man yelled, 'Let me count it, let me count it.'

Kansas ripped the purse from Lynette's hands and threw it to the blonde man, who took the money from it and began counting.

Minutes passed and then, through the dust mask, he cried, 'Seventeen thousand dollars.'

'Whose safe is it?' asked Kansas.

'You don't need to know,' said Lynette.

'It's a woman,' said Cody, and lit a cigarette. 'She's got a condo over on Belmont. I don't know the address but I could get it.'

'Fuck you, Cody,' said Lynette.

Kansas took another can of Hamm's from the refrigerator, opened it and said, 'I'm taking everything that's in the safe. That's it.' Under the fluorescent lights Lynette could see that his nostrils were caked in dried blood and his eyes were bloodshot. He took the five hundred dollars she had given him from his coverall pocket and dropped it on the workbench. 'You can have this back. I'll give Cody the drugs, the silver dollars and the jewellery. I'll let you leave but before you go I want to know whose safe this is. I want to make sure it doesn't come back on me.'

'Like Cody told you, it's just a woman and I know she won't bother you.'

Kansas picked up the four-foot crowbar off the ground. He looked at the man with the blonde hair and snapped his fingers. 'Lock the door because I'm gonna kill her.'

The blonde-haired man ran to the metal door. It was a key-bolt lock; he turned it, took the key out and put it in his pocket. He placed a metal security bar across the door.

'Don't kill her, man,' cried Cody. 'What's the point of that? I mean, I just got out of prison. I can't get involved in anything like this.'

Kansas grabbed Lynette by the hair and forced her to the ground. He pushed her until she was on her back and then straddled her and sat on her chest. 'We'll bleed her in the utility sink and put the rest of her in the acid drum.'

Cody moved further back toward the wood stove and said nothing.

Kansas looked at the blonde man. 'Get my Buck knife from the drawer and the blanket covering the motorcycle. Put the blanket underneath her neck to soak up the blood. I'll cut her throat right here. As soon as I do, get the empty blue drum. We'll drain her blood into it. After that, clean out the concrete sink and make sure to have a strainer over the drain. And take off the mask. We can't have you passing out.'

Lynette was so scared she couldn't speak. Kansas's full weight was on her chest and his legs pinned her arms against the concrete floor. The blonde-haired man brought over the knife and a brown wool blanket. Kansas grabbed her hair, leaned back, taking his weight off her, and pulled her toward him until she was nearly sitting up. The blonde-haired man put the blanket underneath her and then Kansas threw her back down, knocking the wind from her.

'Get the drum now,' he yelled, and looked at Lynette. 'Tell me whose stuff this is.'

Lynette shook her head. 'Please,' she finally whispered. 'Don't kill me, because if you do you'll have to worry about

Cody. And we both know Cody will talk. You'll have to kill him too. And what's the point of killing him? That means you kill two people for seventeen thousand dollars, some jewellery and a bag of drugs you say you don't even want.'

Kansas opened the knife blade and brought it to her neck.

'I can bring you an eighty-thousand-dollar Mercedes,' she said, and began crying.

'What?' said Kansas.

'I have . . . I have a Mercedes I could give you tonight.'

'Why do you have it?'

'I just do.'

'Where?'

'North Portland,' she whispered.

'Why should I believe you?'

'I have the key in my purse. I swear I have it and I'll give it to you. I just took it from a man I know to screw up his night, to be mean. But you can have it if you don't kill me.'

'I'm going to kill you unless you tell me whose safe this is.'

'It's just a woman who I work with,' said Lynette. 'She's not dangerous. She just owed me eight thousand dollars and said she was broke. But I knew she was lying so I took the safe. But I didn't want to steal anything from her, not really. I just want what's mine.'

Kansas stood up and smiled a mouth full of perfect white teeth. Dentures. 'I wasn't going to kill you. I just wanted the truth.' He shut the blade on the knife and set it on the workbench, and to the blonde man said, 'Empty her purse.'

The blonde man poured out Lynette's bag onto the shop table. There was the jewellery, the silver dollars, the papers and photos, the drugs, a pack of mints, hand lotion, tampons, a pack of Kleenex, lip balm, a set of keys, a phone, gum and a single key with a Mercedes emblem.

Kansas picked up the key. 'What kind of Mercedes?'

'It's new, I know that. He just got it. And it's a four-door. A sedan. And it's black.'

Kansas went to the corner of the workbench, where a laptop sat. He turned it on while the blonde-haired man took the dust mask off and sprayed more gas into it.

'It's just a rich guy's car,' said Lynette, and walked slowly toward her purse. 'He's harmless and he won't do anything about it, not really. I can drive Cody to it and he can bring it back to you.'

Cody was still standing behind the wood stove, silent, just looking at them. Kansas rubbed his eyes and again looked at the computer.

'I have photos of the car on my phone. I'll know what model then,' she said, and moved to the workbench. Kansas was trying to type in *Mercedes* but he couldn't spell *Mercedes*. She picked up her phone, moved away from the bench, unlocked it and looked at the signal. Five bars. She dialled 9-1, and then, in a shakier voice, said, 'I've just dialled 9-1. All I have to do is hit 1 and they'll find me.'

'If you do call the police, I really will kill you,' Kansas said, getting up.

'Then you'll go to prison,' said Lynette. 'And the thing that you don't know about me is that I don't care if you kill me. The truth is, I wouldn't mind if you did.'

The blonde-haired man grabbed a box cutter from the shop table and began pacing as he showed Lynette the blade. His breathing grew quicker and quicker until he just stopped and puked into the dust mask. Vomit spilled out the sides and ran down his neck. He was still on his feet when he blacked out and fell, his head hitting the edge of the table on the way down. On the concrete floor he went into a seizure. Kansas ran to him and pulled the mask from his face and Lynette went to the table, grabbed her purse, shoved everything from the safe, including the money, back inside, and headed for the door.

Kansas looked up at Cody in a panic. 'Stop her,' he screamed while the blonde-haired man continued to convulse. White foam frothed from his mouth and blood poured from the cut on his head, a pool of it forming around him on the concrete floor.

Cody didn't move.

'I know about seizures,' Lynette said to Kansas. 'Make sure to put him on his side. You don't want him to choke on his vomit. Get the knife out of his hand too, because he might start thrashing around.'

Kansas only put his fingers in the man's mouth.

'You don't have to do that,' said Lynette. 'He won't swallow his tongue. But he could bite your fingers. He could clamp down on them. Just put him on his side and try to stop the bleeding. You have to get him to the hospital. He could be bleeding in his brain.'

Kansas grew frantic. He began shaking his head with a look of terror on his face. He picked up the man with blonde hair and held him in his arms.

'Get the key to the door from his pocket,' Lynette said to Cody, but Cody was still motionless by the wood stove. She yelled at him: 'He has the key in his fucking pocket. You've got to let him get to the hospital. Do you want him to die?'

Cody looked at her, then slowly went to Kansas and took the key from the blonde man's coverall pocket. He pulled the security bar from across the door and unlocked the bolt.

The blonde-haired man kept spitting white foam from his mouth and Kansas moaned out, 'Oh no, oh no, oh no,' over and over. But even with him in his arms and having a seizure, Kansas went for Lynette's purse. In the struggle he dropped the blonde man hard on the floor and hit Lynette in the stomach. She fell and he put the purse on the blonde man's chest and picked him back up. He headed for the door but the blonde man convulsed so hard that the purse dropped to the ground.

'I'll carry it for you,' said Lynette. 'But you better hurry. He's gonna die if you don't get him to a doctor.'

'But the purse is mine,' cried Kansas. 'It's mine.'

'I know,' said Lynette. 'I know it is.'

Kansas was running with the man in his arms when he hit the right side of the door with the man's leg. The edge of the metal security bar holder went into his calf with such force that it ripped his coveralls and tore a long gash in his leg that instantly leaked out blood. Kansas kept going. He turned left toward the gravel lot and jogged down the path. Lynette grabbed the purse and ran out the door, turning right into complete darkness. She took her phone from her coat pocket, turned on the light and put the strap of her purse round her neck. She ran alongside the building until it ended at the ten-foot chain-link fence and an empty field on the other side.

She started climbing it as the rain came down and slipped twice. She was nearly at the top when Kansas came running back to her. He shook the fence, trying to get her to fall. 'Give me the fucking purse,' he cried in his broken voice. 'Give me the fucking purse.'

Lynette was halfway down the other side when she dropped to the ground. Dogs in nearby yards went crazy with barking and Kansas began going back to where he'd left the blonde man on the wet gravel and was almost to him when he once again turned around. He ran back to the fence and screamed, 'The purse!' but by then Lynette had disappeared into the darkness.

13

The field ended at a paved road and a row of houses. There were no sidewalks and dogs barked from every home she passed. She worked her way back to the derelict house and the shop behind it. At the edge of the property she waited but heard and saw nothing. From her front pocket she took out her car keys, again unlocked her phone, hit 9-1 and began walking down the gravel road. A floodlight was now on and she could see Cody sitting on the trunk of her car in the steady falling rain.

When she was twenty yards away she yelled, 'Where are they?'

'They went to the hospital,' he yelled back. 'Let's get the fuck out of here.'

'You're sure he's gone?'

'He drove off in his truck but he might have called someone. So let's go.'

Lynette ran to her car and they got in. She locked her door, started the car on the fourth try, pulled them onto the street and drove out of the neighbourhood to 82nd Avenue. After a mile she pulled over in front of Ocean City Chinese restaurant.

'Get out of my car,' she told Cody.

'That's bullshit. I ain't getting out.'

'I'm serious. Get out of my car.'

'The buses have quit and it's raining like a motherfucker.

No way I'm getting out. Just give me my cut and a ride back to The Dutchman.'

Lynette wiped the condensation from the windshield and set the rag back on the dash.

She looked at the Chinese restaurant. It was closed but the inside lights were on. The walls and tables were gold, and there were two women vacuuming. Lynette leaned over and opened the glovebox. She grabbed the pint of Jägermeister from it, took a long drink and handed it to Cody. He drank from it and then put the bottle between his legs.

'Just get out, please,' she begged.

'What was I supposed to do?'

Lynette sighed. 'I don't know.'

Cody took another drink. 'Well, there was nothing. I mean, I wasn't going to fight him. I told you he was psycho. And remember, you're the one who wanted to steal the safe, not me. I had nothing to do with it. So just give me my money and take me to The Dutchman.'

Lynette again sighed but steered the car back onto the street.

Cody lit a cigarette. 'What are you going to do with the drugs?'

'I don't know.'

'I could probably sell the package for you.'

'You told Kansas you didn't want them.'

'I don't, I can't even have the shit near my house, but I know some people who could get rid of it pretty easy.'

'I don't think so,' said Lynette.

'Do you know anyone who'd buy that much?'

'I don't even know what it is.'

'At least let me see,' he said.

They came to a stop light and Lynette took the gallon freezer bag from her purse and handed it to Cody. Inside the bag was another bag and he opened it, took a small pinch and put it in his mouth.

'It's coke.'

'I thought it probably was,' said Lynette.

'Why would your friend have that much coke?'

'I don't know.'

Cody took a larger pinch from the package and snorted it off the back of his hand.

'Jesus, what are you doing? I thought you get drug-tested.'

'I do but it's random and they just tested me. I should be alright.' He took another drink from the bottle. 'I really could sell this for you.'

'No way. I don't want anything more to do with you. Just put the package in the glovebox.'

But Cody held on to it and snorted more off his hand. When Lynette turned west on Division Street, he put the package in his hoodie pocket and shut the glovebox.

They drove in silence until she turned right on 48th.

'What about the Mercedes?'

'What do you mean?'

'Was that for real?'

Lynette nodded.

'I could sell that for you too.'

She laughed. 'I'm just gonna drop you off. And take the coke out of your pocket and put it in the glovebox.'

97

'The stuff in the safe is mine as much as it is yours,' he said, and wiped the condensation on the windshield with his arm. 'You couldn't have stole it without my help.' The Dutchman's neon sign came into view. Lynette pulled to the side of the road, the windshield wipers going as fast as they could as the rain hit the hood and roof of the car. She took five hundred dollars from her front pants pocket and handed it to him. 'Give me the package and get out. The five hundred's all I'm giving you because you told him to take whatever he wanted. You guys set me up and when he had me on the floor and I thought he was gonna kill me you didn't do anything. You didn't help at all.'

'Look,' he said, and took a drag from his cigarette, 'I'll be honest. I'm not good when shit gets weird. But I wasn't gonna let you die. I had a plan. You just jumped in before I could do anything. And listen . . . An idea just came to me. I have seven grand at my place. Would you take seven grand for the car? I know a guy who could sell it. You keep my cut and the coke but give me the car and I'll give you seven grand.'

'How do you have seven thousand dollars?'

'When I got out of prison my mother gave me my college fund. Ten grand. I was broke and she knew by then I was never going to go to college so she gave it to me so I wouldn't move in with her. I mean, she has a three-bedroom house off Halsey. Lives by herself in a fucking castle but won't even put me up for a year.' He looked out the window. 'And worse than that, she probably won't even give me the house when she dies. She's crazy for my cousins, sends them to science camp and shit like that. They'll probably get everything.'

'There's no way you have seven grand,' said Lynette.

'I do,' he said, and wiped his nose on his sleeve. 'I really have it.'

'Then why haven't you bought a car if you hate the bus so much?'

'Because I'm just waiting on the right deal. Looking around. But I have the money. I already bought an Xbox and a mountain bike. I'm just trying not to blow it all at once. And I have trouble with my licence too, that's a lot of it but that ain't my fault either. They just fucked me over and took it away. I swear to God I have the money. I rent a room in a house off 160th and Sandy. The money's there and I'll give it to you if you really have the car.'

'I have the car.'

'And whose is it?'

'No one you know.'

'As long as it ain't somebody who'll come back and kill me. Is it that kind of guy?'

'No, he's just a rich old guy, like I told Kansas.'

Cody took a drink of the Jägermeister and set it on the floor in front of him. 'Look, you know it wasn't my fault what Kansas did. I mean, you were there. It wasn't me that pulled the knife on you and it wasn't me who was gonna cut your throat. Maybe he and I talked about taking more than what we'd agreed on, but we were just talking. To me a deal's a deal. You and me had a plan and I was gonna stick to it no matter what. And in the end Kansas wouldn't have gotten shit but his five hundred. That's the truth. And look.' He took Kansas's Buck knife from his pocket. 'When shit got crazy with the blonde dude, I stole the knife. I would have fucked him up. It just wasn't time yet. But I'm a go-to person and you know it. I mean, you needed a guy to open the safe and I found that guy. It got weird, sure, but that's just the way it goes sometimes. The price of doing business. But you came to me and I got the safe opened. So really, I've done everything you've asked. There was just a little drama, sure, but we got out of it. So give me the car and I'll give you the money. I'm on the bus three hours a day to work a shitty job at a shitty restaurant. I mean, they really fuck people getting out of prison. The Mercedes could be a good turning point for me 'cause I know a guy who is a Mercedes mechanic, and he'll have no problem getting rid of it. So I give you my word and my word's good. I'll give you the money if you give me the car.'

'Then give me back the cocaine first.'

'Alright,' he said, and took the package from his hoodie pocket and handed it to her.

★

At the edge of Gresham was a 1970s single-storey ranch house at the end of a cul-de-sac. Two cars and a truck were parked in the driveway and no lights were on. Lynette pulled behind a lifted black Dodge pickup and left her car running. On the back windshield was a large decal of a skull wearing a German helmet and on the bumper was a sticker that read *Kick Their Ass Take Their Gas.* Cody opened the passenger-side door, got out and ran inside.

Five minutes passed but he didn't come back. Lynette

grew more and more anxious and pulled onto the street. With the engine running and the lights off, she got out of the car and opened the trunk. Underneath the spare tyre she put the seventeen thousand dollars, the cocaine, the jewellery, the photos and the papers, then got back in and locked the doors. Five more minutes passed and she was about to leave when Cody came jogging out from the side of the house wearing a red hoodie. She unlocked the passenger-side door and he got in.

'What took you so long?' she asked.

'I had to do a few things first.'

'Like what?'

'I had to change clothes. I was wet as shit.'

'That took you almost ten minutes?'

'And I was on the can and I couldn't get off, okay? Is that good enough? Coke always fucks up my guts.'

'Do you have the money?'

'I have it,' he said.

'Let me see it.'

'Don't worry, I got it.'

'If you don't let me count it right now you can get out. There's no way I'm trusting you.'

Cody sneered but reached into his hoodie pocket and pulled out a white US Bank envelope. Lynette turned on the overhead light, took the envelope from him and counted the money.

'There's only five thousand here.'

'I told you, I bought a bike and an Xbox. And I needed to keep some to cover my rent. I mean, I have to keep my room. My parole will get fucked up if I don't have a real place to stay, so you can't ask me to risk that money too. That's going too far.'

He took the envelope from her and put it back in his hoodie pocket, and she began driving. She took I-84 west into the city, crossed the Fremont Bridge and went along Highway 30. The St Johns Bridge came into view and she took it back over the river into North Portland. They didn't talk until they saw the Mercedes underneath a street lamp across from the closed-down Tulip Pastry Shop.

'There it is,' she said, and parked. She took the key from her purse and showed him.

Cody wiped his nose on his sleeve. 'It's real,' he said, and grinned.

'Give me the money and I'll give you the key.'

'It better be the right key.'

'It is.'

He looked out the window at the Mercedes. 'It's brand new, isn't it?'

'I think so. I don't know how many miles are on it but he hasn't had it long. So just give me the money and get out.'

'How about you throw in the cocaine too.'

'No,' she said. 'The key for the money. That was the deal.'

Cody kept his eyes on the Mercedes. He took the envelope out of his hoodie pocket.

'It better open the door.'

'It does. I'm gonna hit the Open button on the key.' She did, and across the street the car lit up.

'Goddamn,' he said, and then suddenly lunged for the key and grabbed it. He put it in his hoodie pocket and went for the purse that sat on the floor underneath Lynette's legs. He had it in his right hand but he couldn't get it out because the strap was around her left ankle. As he pulled on it she hit him in the face. He let go of the purse and came after her. He put his hands around her throat and pressed so hard she couldn't breathe. He was strangling her. Lynette tried to pull his hands off her neck but he was too strong and she was jammed against the driver's-side door, unable to move. She started to panic and tried desperately to move her feet from under the steering wheel, but couldn't. She began hitting him on the side of the head but he wouldn't stop squeezing. With her left hand she grabbed his hair and pulled on it as hard as she could. He screamed and took his hands from her throat and hit her in the stomach, but by then she'd got her feet up from under the steering wheel and she began kicking him. She got his face twice and that stopped him. He opened the passenger-side door and got out.

As he staggered back into the street Lynette found Kenny's old Portland Beavers mini-bat on the floor of the back seat, grabbed it, got out of the car and ran to him. 'Give me the fucking key back,' she yelled. But Cody was holding Kansas's Buck knife. The blade was out and pointing toward her.

'You'd really stab me?' she said. 'You'd kill a person for a car?'

'If you make me stab you, I will.'

'Just give me the money and take the car. That was the deal.'

'I ain't giving you the money,' he said, and a thin line of

blood ran from his nose down over his upper lip. 'I need that money.'

She tried to think and then finally said, 'Okay. I don't want to get stabbed. I'll leave, but just so you know, you have the wrong key. It's a key to a Saab. I have the right key in my pocket. I hit that one at the same time I hit the one I gave you.'

A panic fell across Cody's face and he took the key from his pocket and glanced at it for just a moment, and when he did, Lynette hit him on the side of the neck with the bat. He dropped the knife and the key and fell to the ground and she began to beat him. He cried out for her to stop but she didn't stop. She hit him more than a dozen times. By the end he was sobbing. His mouth and nose were pouring out blood and he was curled into a ball. When she quit he was still breathing but he wasn't moving. She took the envelope from his pocket, picked up the knife, closed the blade and put it in her coat pocket. She looked at the licence plate of the Mercedes, memorized the number and got back in her car, locked the doors, started the engine, and waited.

Minutes passed and she stared at Cody on the asphalt under the street lamp, not moving. She was about to call for an ambulance when he sat up and slowly stood. He spat on the ground and felt his face, then looked around until he found the Mercedes key. He opened the driver's-side door, got in and started the engine. The headlights came on and she watched him drive off.

14

The Original Hotcake House was a twenty-four-hour restaurant. It was 3 a.m. and inside was empty but for three drunk men in their early twenties eating breakfast. She ordered a Denver omelette and a cup of coffee at the counter, went to the bathroom and locked the door.

She took her scarf and coat off and looked at herself in the mirror. There were red marks on her neck from Cody's hands but they weren't as bad as she'd thought they would be. Her stomach was sore from the punches but her face was untouched. She washed it, put her scarf and coat back on and went out. She sat on the opposite side of the restaurant from the men and after a few minutes her order came up.

As a kid, she'd been taken to the Hotcake House by her grandfather countless times. It had been his favourite restaurant. He was a handsome thickset man with huge forearms and shoulders and short grey hair. He worked as a union stevedore for forty years and wore the same thing every day: Levi's, work boots and a Ben Davis pinstriped half-zipper shirt. From when she was a baby Lynette would spend three weekends a month with her grandmother and grandfather in St Johns. When she grew older her grandfather would wake her before dawn, put shoes on her feet and a jacket over her pyjamas, and carry her to his truck. He would then drive them to the Hotcake House for breakfast.

Afterward he'd take them to Portland Meadows horse track to watch the early-morning workouts. Her grandfather would carry her in one arm and hold a kids' sleeping bag and a thermos of coffee in the other. He'd lay the sleeping bag out on a bench and she'd get in and watch the horses working out while her head rested on her grandfather's leg. She would fall in and out of sleep for what seemed like hours. The smell of coffee from his thermos, the sound of the horses running, and her warm inside the sleeping bag.

Her grandfather took her everywhere, to the movies, to the hardware store and the auto parts store. When he met his friends for coffee she'd be there, and when he went to the stock car races in St Helens or the hockey games at Memorial Coliseum, when he bought new clothes at Jower's or The Man's Shop, or ate Mexican food or Chinese food or when he got his hair cut at Wayne's Barber Shop. He was proud of her and always introduced her as 'the greatest kid of all time'. He was good to her, always kind, and he gave Lynette her only real break from Kenny. He gave her a chance to just be herself and to be loved for it. But her time with her grandparents ended when she was nine. Her grandfather had dropped his truck off one morning to be repaired and was walking home on Lombard Street when he collapsed on the sidewalk and died of a heart attack. Her grandmother, already in ill health, moved to Yakima and lived in a retirement home with her sister.

As Lynette grew older she went back to the Hotcake House. At thirteen or fourteen, if she had a free Saturday or Sunday, she would take the bus across town just to eat there and think about her grandfather. She told no one about it, about how important the place was to her, until she met Jack. After that she and Jack would go there and she would tell him about her grandfather because she knew they would have been friends. Her grandfather would have been proud of her for being with a man like Jack.

Tears leaked down her face as she ate. What would her grandfather think of her now? After all the horrible things she'd been a part of, the horrible things that she had done herself, or let be done to her. It nearly made her fall to the floor just thinking about it. And for the last three years she'd even failed Kenny. What would her grandfather think of that? Of her ignoring him the way she had. Sleep and work and trying to save money to buy the house. Three years without looking up once. It had strained them all. Her mother and Kenny had both become depressed, had both gained weight, and her mother smoked too much and had begun drinking more. And now they wouldn't even have a home of their own. She had failed.

As she ate her omelette and drank her coffee she knew that she was ruled by guilt. She had been broken by her brother because, after her grandfather died, her life as Kenny's sister had changed to her life as Kenny's caregiver. On weekdays, before she'd got on at Fred Meyer Jewelers, her mother had been a dinner waitress at Elmer's Restaurant in Delta Park. Lynette, still only nine, would look after Kenny during her mother's shifts. They'd be locked inside the house so they couldn't get out. Two key-only bolt locks on the front and back doors.

By twelve, Lynette would get Kenny up before school, dress him, make his breakfast and pack his lunch. In the afternoon, when her classes finished, she'd go to Kenny's school and bring him home on a city bus. When they were able to get seats, Kenny had to be on the inside or he would try to escape. If they had to stand she would hold his hand as tight as she could when the bus driver came to a stop. If she wasn't paying attention, if she wasn't holding on to him hard enough, he'd break free and run for the exit. She'd have to yell at the driver to leave the door open and she'd run off too and chase him down the street.

By thirteen, she made his dinners: canned soup or macaroni and cheese or scrambled eggs or frozen pizzas. She cleaned his room and the bathroom where he made daily messes and never once, during all those years, was he the brunt of her growing anger and anguish. As she sat there now she was at least proud of that.

What haunted her, however, was that she'd ignored him. She'd spent years just trying to distract him in any way she could think of to get relief, to get some time to herself. She fed him too much, left him in front of the TV too often, and when he was really difficult she slipped him a Benadryl and put him to bed. In high school she'd sometimes left him alone. She would lock him in his bedroom and go to parties or go to movies with friends. Afterward she would rush home before her mother got off work and calm Kenny with Pop-Tarts and cookies and movies. She'd dote on him while frantically cleaning his room so her mother would never know she had locked him inside it.

But she also knew that, for years, she and her mother

had tried. They'd taken him to whatever programmes they could get him into, worked on socializing him, followed any and all advice from teachers, therapists, doctors, nurses and specialists.

When Lynette was fourteen and her brother sixteen, he was accepted to summer art camp just south of Coos Bay, on a need-based scholarship. Her mother had planned that after they dropped him off she and Lynette would take their first family vacation. For two nights they rented a cabin near Port Orford. They took walks on the beach, ate Mexican food and lay on the sand and read books side by side. The third and fourth nights they spent in San Francisco, where they stayed at a motel in Chinatown. They took tourist pictures, her mother bought Lynette a sweater, she bought them matching scarves, they rode a cable car and ate in Chinese and Italian restaurants. They held each hour like escaped convicts who knew they were soon to be taken back. They didn't fight, they didn't even bicker, they were for those few days almost friends. Because they were, for the first time, free. It was the longest Lynette had been away from Kenny in her life and the longest her mother had been away from Kenny since his birth.

On the ride home, with Kenny in the front seat and Lynette in the back, her mother drove them up I-5 and smoked cigarette after cigarette, holding it next to the crack in the driver's-side window and quietly crying to herself. They returned to Portland and were the same. They struggled and they tried for Kenny, and then her mother met Randy and after three months of dating he moved in. They kept trying even then, until Randy broke into the bathroom while Lynette was in the tub and she ran away from home at sixteen.

★

Two drunk couples came into the Hotcake House and sat across from Lynette, so she finished her coffee, left half of the omelette on her plate and got up. It was 3.40 a.m. and outside it seemed to be raining even harder. Her car started on the second try and she drove across the Ross Island Bridge, made her way back to the Hotel deLuxe and used the key card she'd kept in her purse to get back into room 315. Inside, she took off her coat and scarf, sat on the bed and picked up the phone. She left a voice message with the 9th Street Bakery explaining that she couldn't come in for the rest of the week. Next she called the police non-emergency line and left a message.

'I'm staying at the Hotel deLuxe,' she said, 'and I was parked on the street. I was going to my car when I saw a man break the driver's-side window of a Mercedes and get in. The man was really tall. I'd guess around six-three or -four. He was white and skinny. He had a patchy beard and really bright-coloured tattoos on his arms. There was another man with him but he didn't get into the car. He just ran away. But before he took off I heard him say, "Don't fuck up the ignition, Cody." It was a black Mercedes four-door. Oregon licence plate, 924-DVC. Here's the thing, though – when the man drove off I followed him. He went to a shop in the back of a white house on Con Littin Road, off Johnson Creek. There was a sign on the property that said *Johnson Creek Auto Repair*. The man dropped the Mercedes off there and got into another car and drove to 14899 Graham Park Place. It's off 160th and Sandy Boulevard. My name is Phyllis Waterson, room 315.'

She found a phone number for the Parole & Probation Department in Portland. The offices were also closed but she left another message. 'Hello,' she said. 'I'm calling to report that my brother, Cody Henson, who was an inmate in the prison in Pendleton, has been drinking and doing cocaine. I think he stole a car too, a black Mercedes, Oregon licence plate, 924-DVC. I'm worried about his safety. I think he'll harm himself and maybe others. He needs help. My name is Gloria Henson. My brother works at The Dutchman in Southeast Portland, off Hawthorne. Thank you and please help him before he does something really bad.'

When she hung up she left the room and took the stairs down to the lobby. She got back in her car and dialled another number. It rang six times before a young woman answered.

'Sorry to call so late,' said Lynette. 'But JJ used to stay up all night and I thought maybe he still did.'

'His TV's still on,' the woman said. 'I think he's still up. Who's this?'

'Can you tell him it's Lynette and it's really important?'

The woman put down the phone and Lynette took Kenny's sleeping bag from the back seat, covered herself with it and waited until a man's voice came on the phone.

'Hello?' he said uncertainly.

'This is Lynette.'

'Lynette?'

'Yeah.'

'You're still living in Portland?'

'Yeah.'

'I thought you were long gone.'

'No.'

'Why are you calling me at four fifteen in the morning? I haven't talked to you in, what, almost seven years?'

'Something like that. It's been a long time.'

'What do you want?'

'Do you still sell cocaine?'

'Why would you ask that?'

'I came across a package of it and I want to sell it.'

She could hear him light a cigarette. 'Why tonight and why me?'

'Because I don't know anyone else. I don't even know anyone who does it and you used to sell it. Tonight because if I don't do it now I'll lose my nerve and just throw it away. But I think I'm leaving town and I want all the money I can get. I don't need to make much off it so it'll probably be a good deal for you.'

'Where did you get it?'

'I just kind of stumbled upon it. No one knows I have it and I haven't told anyone about it. And it's no one dangerous I got it from. No one like that at all. Are you interested?'

'I don't have a ton of cash on me.'

'You used to always have a lot of cash on you.'

He was silent for nearly a minute and then said, 'Come over but don't bring anyone else – just you, okay?'

'Okay,' she said, and hung up.

15

At Cully and 62nd Lynette took a side street where the asphalt turned to gravel and she hit potholes and water splashed under the wheel wells and twice the car bottomed out. When she came to the house where she'd lived for eleven months when she was sixteen, she parked the car, shut off the headlights and engine, and knew what she was doing was a mistake. She closed her eyes and waited until the song playing on the radio ended, then got out of the car and headed toward the front door.

★

There was a rundown vintage thrift shop on Alberta Street that Lynette used to stop by on the two Saturdays each month that her mother let her have to herself. She was a freshman in high school at the time, and the owner, a forty-two-year-old man named JJ Benada, noticed her. He gave her free clothes if she helped in the store for the afternoon. Sometimes he'd order pizza and have her pick it up down the street and they'd eat together. He paid attention to her, told her she was beautiful, told her jokes and made her laugh, and always he had a movie playing on a TV behind the counter and a beer going that he'd drink out of a coffee cup. After a while he even let her sit behind the counter with him. He taught her to use the register, taught her how to price clothes, and began inviting her to parties and gigs that she was never able to attend.

When she ran away, the first thing she thought of was money. She needed a job so she went to the vintage shop and asked JJ for one. Even now she could remember herself standing in front of him in tears one afternoon, telling him she had nowhere to live, and how he'd stepped out from behind the counter and hugged her. When the store closed that evening he brought her to his house, got them Mexican food, found her a sleeping bag and a bath towel and gave her the couch.

For eleven months she learned to drink, smoke weed and do cocaine in that house. And it was there she lost her virginity to JJ and slept with other men, and a woman too. It was also where she first fell apart, where her anger finally erupted, where she lost ten pounds, had hives on her back and spiralled into her first depression.

The house itself was single-storey and painted dark purple. Security lights came on and lit the property as she walked up. The yard was overgrown, abandoned to grass, weeds and blackberry bushes. The shrubs and trees next to the house nearly blocked it from view.

A pregnant girl answered the front door dressed in pink sweats and black-and-white slippers with panda heads sewn on the toes. Her hair was short and dyed blonde. Her arms and legs were so thin and long that she looked anorexic, yet her chest and neck were so thick they looked nearly compressed. She had a pushed-up nose and sad green eyes.

'I'm the one that just called,' said Lynette. 'JJ said it was okay to come by.'

The girl smiled. 'And you're alone, right? He said to make sure you're alone.'

'I'm alone.'

'Well, then come in. He's in his bedroom. Do you know where it is?'

Lynette nodded and went inside.

There was no heat on and she could see her breath as she entered. The living room still had the same threadbare brown carpet and the same two black couches that formed an L in the corner of the room. The long tile coffee table was in its usual place and on it were stacks of *Us* and *People* magazines, a jar of weed and an ornate glass bong. A large flat-screen TV hung from the far wall. The TV was new but the posters around it were the ones she remembered. Band posters: The Wipers, Dead Moon, Caustic Soda, Napalm Beach, The Jackals and Poison Idea.

The pregnant girl moved back to the couch, took a drink from a plastic bottle of Pepsi and put a comforter over herself. A Harry Potter movie was paused on the TV and she started it again. The hall was dark but a line of light came from underneath a door at the end of it. Lynette went to it, knocked, and a man's voice told her to come in. Warm air rushed out as she entered. Inside, the walls were painted flat black and the ceiling a glossy dark red. Another TV hung from the wall. Two portable electric oil heaters were on each side of a king-sized bed, where JJ lay underneath a black bedspread.

'Shut the door,' he coughed. 'Don't let the heat out.'

She closed it while he sat up in bed and smiled stained yellow teeth. He wore no shirt and his arms and chest were covered in faded tattoos. Dyed shoulder-length black hair hung down around his thick-rimmed glasses.

'You look good,' he said, and got out of bed. He was naked and skinny with only a small gut. His skin had begun to sag and his legs and groin were covered in indiscernible old black-ink tattoos. He dressed, put on a winter coat, and they left the room.

In the kitchen JJ took a beer from the refrigerator, opened a cupboard and pulled out a scale. He then told Lynette to follow him down the stairs to the basement, where he turned on a series of lights and Lynette saw that even the basement hadn't changed since she'd lived there. The walls were painted black and half-covered with local band posters and flyers from twenty-five years ago: Calamity Jane, Pond, Crackerbash, The Maroons, Oblivion Seekers, Vehicle, The Obituaries. A collection of stained carpet remnants and rugs covered the concrete floor and it smelled of stale beer and mould and incense. There was a wet bar in the corner of the room and he went behind it, sat on a stool and lit a cigarette.

Lynette sat across from him on another stool, took out the freezer bag of cocaine and set it on the bar. JJ picked it up and put it on the scale.

'You have more than a half of a kilo here,' he said.

'How much is that worth?'

'Six grand, maybe. Can I try it?'

Lynette nodded.

JJ got up from the stool and came back with a small mirror, a library card and a four-inch straw, and snorted two lines.

'Is it any good?' she asked.

He opened the can of beer and nodded. 'Where did you get it?'

'I just sorta stumbled upon it,' she said. 'Will you buy it?'

He shook his head. 'Me, I can't.'

Up close, Lynette could see he had become an old man. His dyed black hair was brittle and looked like a wig. His face had become wrinkled, his eyelids drooped, and the stubble on his face was grey.

'I can't have it around me. You meet the girl upstairs?'

'She having your kid?'

He nodded.

'Where did you find her?'

'She works for me.'

'Poor gal,' said Lynette.

JJ took another drink and pinched his nose with his fingers. 'Don't come to my house in the middle of the night and say shit like that. Remember, you called me. I've never once tried to find you. You can leave if you're gonna be a bitch.' He took more cocaine out of the bag.

'I'm sorry,' she said. 'I shouldn't have said that.'

He shook his head and began chopping lines. 'You're the one driving around in the middle of the night with a half a kilo of coke, calling someone you say you hate.'

She nodded and watched as he cut the lines.

'I'm not at your house, am I? You think I did you so wrong but you know I never wanted you to live here in the first place. You begged your way in and I let you stay as charity.'

'I know.'

'I didn't kidnap you, did I?'

'No.'

'Did I rape you?'

'No.'

'So don't look at me like I did,' he said. 'That was over thirteen years ago when we were together.'

'I'm not looking at you in any way.'

'Bullshit. I know that look because I know you. You despise me, you hate my fucking guts. But remember, you're the one who came to my shop and hung around. You're the one who begged me for a job. Begged and begged and begged.'

Lynette nodded. 'I know I did. I get it. But I was just a kid. So back off. I just want to sell this stuff.'

He did another line and then looked at her. 'And you came on to me. I didn't come on to you, did I?'

'I don't want to talk about this.'

'Did I come on to you?'

'No, but I was desperate.'

'I know you were,' he said, and leaned back and laughed. 'That's why I didn't do anything. I put you on the couch in the front room. I did it to give you a break. To help you because it was winter and you said you didn't have any place to live. Did I ask anything of you? Expect anything? Did I make a move on you?'

'No,' she said.

'And I tried to figure out where you came from, where you lived, who you lived with. Even before you stayed here, when you were just hanging around the store, I never knew anything about you. I tried but you wouldn't talk. And then after two weeks on the couch you're the one who came back naked and crawled in bed with me. Am I lying about that?'

'No,' she said. 'But I was scared that if I didn't sleep with you, you'd get tired of me. That you'd kick me out and I didn't know where else to go. Everyone said that about you.'

'Who?'

'Just girls around your store.'

'That's bullshit. That's your thinking, not mine.'

'Maybe . . . But I was just a kid. I was really messed up.'

'And now you're not?' he said. 'Now you're driving around with a bagful of coke in your coat pocket, showing up before dawn to a guy's house you haven't seen in almost seven years.'

'Maybe,' she whispered.

'And let's be honest for a second. You fucked me over more than I fucked you over.'

Lynette laughed. 'You're a piece of shit for saying that. You've always been an asshole on cocaine.'

JJ shrugged and took another drink of beer.

'Are you going to buy it?'

'I'm not sure yet.'

She stared at him.

'You're still an angry bitch.'

'Maybe – maybe I am. Maybe just seeing you pisses me off. And memories of this place. Maybe it's that . . . How many girls that come around your store have you ended up with? You groom vulnerable girls. That's what you do.'

'I haven't groomed anybody for anything. That's bullshit.' He let out a short laugh and took a drink of beer. 'I wasn't the one that got you pregnant, was I? And who paid for your abortion, huh? Did your so-called "fiancé"? Where the fuck was he? Where were your parents or your real friends then? Why didn't you go to them if you hated me so much? Why come crawling back to me for help? I hadn't seen you in five or six years and then you call out of the blue. I sure wasn't the devil then. I didn't ask questions, didn't give you a hard time, I just helped you. I drove you there, paid for it and let you crash on my couch for a couple days to recover. So don't unload a bunch of shit on me 'cause your life's falling apart. Look, I gave you a place to stay when you were homeless. I gave you a job and money and fed you. I was the best thing in your life and you know it.'

'I was just a kid.'

'You weren't that much of a kid.'

Lynette paused for a moment. 'You made me sleep with those guys.'

'I didn't make you. I didn't force you.'

'You did in your own way. You know that.'

He sipped his beer and nodded. His voice became quiet and trailed off. 'Maybe . . . Maybe I did.'

'And you took pictures of me and filmed us together. I was too young and insecure to know I didn't want that. But I didn't want that.'

Again he nodded.

'And then that one guy. The hairy guy from Seattle. That time you did force me. I begged you that I didn't want to sleep with him but you said I had to. That you'd kick me out if I didn't.'

'That was different,' he whispered, and shook his head. 'I am sorry for that.'

'I tried to kill myself that night.'

'I know.' He looked down at the bar and chopped another line with the library card.

'If it wasn't for that guy, I would have been dead. He came back down to the basement and found me with the empty bottle of Valium. He was the one who cared. He made me puke and stayed with me all night, not you. I just want to know why you would make me do that.'

'He had a serious thing for you . . . And I owed him money. I fucked you over to get out of a bill. I feel horrible about it, but look, I was going through a rough time. Anyway, don't blame me too much. You knew by the first month of living here who I was. You weren't some naive kid so don't say you were. You just needed a place to stay and I gave it to you. And I put up with you. I sure as shit didn't know how unstable you were. But then I didn't know anything about you. You knew Portland and you'd hung around my shop so I figured you were from here but I wasn't positive. I just knew you had a brother. He was the only one you'd talk about. You'd cry about how you missed your brother. I remember that.'

She only nodded and looked at the bar in front of her. It had been the first time in her life she'd lived apart from Kenny and there'd been nights when she couldn't sleep because she missed her brother to the point where her stomach was always sick. Sometimes in the afternoons she would disappear from JJ's store and go to Kenny's school. She would wait until his classes were over and stay with him until Marsha, the woman who took care of him in the afternoons, arrived. Sometimes Marsha would let them have time alone on the school grounds. It wasn't until years later that Lynette learned her mother had paid Marsha to sit in the car and let Lynette and Kenny be together. Marsha would then report back to Doreen how Lynette looked. She would even try to take pictures of Lynette with her phone.

JJ pinched his nose and took a drink of beer. 'I can't take back anything I did – I wish I could. But if you think about it you're the one that set it in motion, not me. You crawled in my bed, I didn't crawl in yours. And you knew how to seduce. You did, because you're good-looking and you knew the power of that. Even then you knew how to use it. At least admit that?'

'I did hit on you, but I thought I loved you.'

'That's bullshit.' He laughed again and lit another cigarette from the pack on the bar. He couldn't sit still any more. 'Let's just be honest for a second. I had things you wanted and we hit it off. And once we got together we had a good eight or nine months. I broke up with Mindy and kicked her out for you.'

'But then you tried to destroy me,' said Lynette. 'You made me feel like I was the most important person in your life and then suddenly you kicked me out of your room and I ended up in the basement. You didn't even tell me why. You didn't explain anything at all. You just made me sleep down here. And then you brought in that other girl. The big one.'

'Martha.'

'Yeah, Martha . . . You didn't tell me anything and all of a sudden she was there and you'd barely talk to me. You'd barely even look at me. Where before we'd go out, suddenly only you and Martha would go out. And I could hear you two upstairs. I could hear you guys in bed. I could hear you two watching TV and laughing. And during the day, at the store, you guys would whisper around me and giggle, like the joke was always on me. Like I was the worst person in the world, like I was nothing. Like just one day I'm a leper.'

JJ shrugged. 'What was I supposed to do? You were having meltdowns. You needed to be on medication. I got tired of you hurting yourself when I didn't pay attention to you. After a while I was just sick of it. I needed to move on.'

Tears welled in Lynette's eyes and she didn't speak for nearly a minute. 'The reason I quit eating and tried to kill myself wasn't just because of that guy. It was because you were so mean to me. I even slept with Martha for you. I did whatever you wanted. Whatever. I did so many things that made me feel bad about myself . . . If you hated me, why not just break up with me or abandon me? Drive me downtown and drop me off. Kick me out of your house and change the locks. I mean, you had just turned forty-four. I remember that. We had that big party for you and you wore a Dallas Cowboys jersey with the number forty-four on it . . . You were a grown man. Look, I'm not an easy person to be around but I didn't know that. Because it started here, or at least showed itself . . . I can be awful . . . That's true. You're not the first person who's said that and I've fucked up a lot of things in my life because of it. But back then it was the only way I knew how to get control of my life. And my life was out of control. But the thing is, I tried hard for you. I did everything. I cooked and did your laundry and I did whatever you wanted when we were together. I did all that 'cause I was an insecure kid, sure, but also because I wanted to make you happy. You were the most important person in my life.'

JJ put two fingers into the cocaine and took out another small pile. He divided it into three lines and snorted them.

When he'd finished she grabbed the package, sealed it and put it back in her coat. 'I don't want to be here any more. Do you want to buy this or not?'

He leaned back and again pinched his nose. 'No . . . Like I said, I can't. But I have a friend who might want to buy it. He's the only guy I know who would have the money and would want it.'

'I'm gonna leave town tomorrow,' she said.

'What time is it?'

Lynette looked at her phone. 'Almost five.'

'He works nights. He's probably still up. I'll text him right now.' JJ put out his cigarette, found his phone in the pocket of his coat, sent a text and then stood up.

'How old's your girlfriend?'

'Eighteen.'

'And you wanted to get her pregnant?'

He nodded. 'My mom's helping put in a playroom down here next month. We'll put in carpet and fix the bathroom, paint it, make it kidproof.' He finished the beer and put his cigarette in the can. 'I'm gonna get another beer. You want one?'

'No,' she said.

'Hold tight and we'll see if this guy texts back,' he said, and went up the stairs.

Ten minutes passed and then she heard footsteps in the kitchen. JJ's phone rang and she could just hear him talking for a time. When the call ended he came down the stairs and again sat across from her at the bar. He had a beer in one hand and a file folder in the other.

'You should take these. I don't want them any more.' He handed her the folder.

'What is it?'

He shrugged.

Lynette opened the folder to see pictures of herself. They were eight-by-ten colour photos. The top one was a close-up of her giving JJ a blowjob. His face wasn't in the photo, only hers. She remembered the night because it was just after her seventeenth birthday and her hair was short and blonde. JJ had given her a birthday coupon to Supercuts to have her hair cut short and dyed blonde. She looked at the other pictures of herself with JJ and pictures of herself with the girl, Martha. None of it really hurt her until she came to a dozen photos of herself trying to pose like she was in a porn magazine. She was on JJ's bed, in the kitchen and in the basement. Her face was so young, her chin covered in acne. She was wearing a necklace her mother had given her, a brown seashell connected to a gold chain, and on her right hand was a silver ring of her grandmother's.

'Did you delete the files?' she asked, and put the photos back in the folder, bent it in half and pushed it into her purse.

He shrugged and took a long drink off the can of beer.

She wiped her eyes and stood up. 'I'm gonna go now.'

'My friend, Rodney, called back. He's interested and said he would buy it for three grand. He said he didn't have any more cash on him so that's his offer. You can go to his house at six, in about forty-five minutes. You want his address?'

Lynette wiped her eyes again. 'And he's alright?'

'He's good enough. He's just one of those guys who's never outgrown cocaine.'

They went upstairs and into the kitchen. JJ opened the fridge and took out another beer. In the living room they could hear Harry Potter on the TV and see the eyes of the pregnant girl lying on her side watching it.

'I'll tell you his address on one condition,' said JJ.

'What's that?'

He moved right next to her and his voice fell quiet. 'If I give you the address I want your word that you'll never come back here. Not ever again. No calls, nothing. I'm gonna be a father soon.'

16

The rain continued and the clock on the dashboard said 5.20 a.m. Her car started on the fifth try and she drove to Prescott and headed north on 60th. For thirteen years she had avoided JJ's neighbourhood the best she could. If she had to drive near it, down Cully or Prescott to get somewhere, just the names alone would unsettle her. She avoided the grocery store he used to go to, the part of Alberta Street where his vintage shop was, the taqueria he had once liked, the Dairy Queen, the liquor store, the Thai place, the barbecue joint, and she never went into any of the bars or clubs she knew he'd liked.

She pulled in at Jubitz Truck Stop and set the file with the photos on the passenger seat. One by one, she took them out, tore them into little pieces and put them back in the file, then got out. She dropped the photos in the first trash can she came to and went into the restaurant, sat at the empty counter and ordered coffee.

It had been nearly seven years since she'd been there. Even Jubitz haunted her. Half the city now seemed to haunt her. At least once a month she, Jack and Kenny had eaten breakfast at Jubitz so that Kenny could watch the semitrucks come and go. Sometimes Jack would get his boots worked on at the shoe repair or they'd take Kenny to movies in the small truck stop theatre.

What would Jack think if he saw those pictures of her?

Or of her being a prostitute or stealing a car and having a bag of cocaine in her purse? She wiped her face with a napkin and took off her scarf and coat. She poured cream and sugar into the cup and stirred it. Even after almost seven years she still missed Jack, and not a day went by where she didn't worry about what he would think of her if he knew her now.

Outside of her grandparents, her brother and mother, Jack was the only person she had ever really loved and he was the only person, outside of her family, who had ever loved her. The only person in the world who had chosen to live with her, chosen to care for her, and taken the chance of loving her.

She'd been twenty-one and working the counter at the Tulip Pastry Shop on Lombard Street when she first met him. Jack Burns was twenty-four and came in one morning on his way to work as a forklift driver for Driscoll Steel Company. He told her later on that when he walked into the bakery that first morning he knew he was seeing the best-looking woman he'd ever meet in his life. She stopped him in his tracks. Lynette felt the same about him. Even after their first encounter she couldn't stop thinking about him because Jack reminded her of her grandfather.

He began coming in regularly and flirting with her and trying to make her laugh, and she in turn would flirt with him and try to make him laugh. They made a game out of everything. After two weeks she bought him a gift: a tin of Badger Balm for Hardworking Hands, because she'd noticed his hands were rough and cracked. It was spring but she wrapped it in Christmas paper. She drew a heart under his name. The place was full of customers when she handed it to him, but he didn't leave after he got his pastry and coffee. He just sat in the back, near the window, and waited. Customer after customer came and went but he didn't leave. An hour passed and then finally, for a moment, the bakery was empty.

'Aren't you late for work?' she asked from behind the counter.

'I called and told them my truck broke down,' he said. 'I just wanted to say thanks.'

'You already thanked me.'

'I know. I just wanted to again.'

'You're welcome.'

'My hands feel better already.'

She laughed. 'I'm glad.'

'Can I see you sometime outside of here?'

'Yes.'

'Tonight?'

'Yes.'

It began. She saw him that evening and almost every evening thereafter for three years. Her life had seen so much darkness before Jack, but in meeting him it was like she was relieved of it. Like she had been saved from herself and her past and suddenly swept away to somewhere beautiful. Her anger vanished to the point where she couldn't remember what it felt like to be full of rage. Her hopelessness disappeared. This is what true love must be, she told herself. It saves you and changes you. It's like living inside a movie where the dirt in you and the scars on you are eradicated.

She slept with him after seven dates. He asked her if she'd had sex before, and she told him only once when she was in high school. She didn't tell him about her past, about running away or about JJ. She didn't tell him about trying to kill herself or the time she'd spent in the psychiatric ward of the hospital. All the things she had done before Jack, the things she was so ashamed of and damaged by, seemed to fade into nothing by just seeing his face. Some nights she'd wake up in his apartment with his arms around her and be so excited and relieved to be free of herself that she would weep.

Within four months she was spending three nights a week at his apartment and she started taking birth control. They had sex nearly every time they saw each other and for the first time in her life she had orgasms. When she stayed at his place he would wake her up with a cup of coffee. He would walk her to work at six and pick her up after she got off. He spent all his money on her and after five months he told her he loved her. He told her he wanted to marry her someday.

Jack had a pickup truck and each week when he got paid he took her out to eat in a different part of town. They saw movies together, they got drunk together and saw bands play. They went roller-skating at Oaks Park and ice-skating at the Lloyd Center. They walked in and out of high-end downtown stores. They spent weekend afternoons strolling through neighbourhoods looking at houses they wanted to live in. They went to furniture stores and picked out the furniture that would go in those houses.

After eight months he drove her to Seaside for the day to meet his parents and then to Eugene, where his brother Henry was taking classes at the community college to be a mechanic. There was a gentleness to Jack that she could just disappear into. Never once did he blindside her or intentionally try to hurt her. He could get nervous or grumpy, insecure or angry, but when he did he would try to talk to her about it. He would try to explain himself to her, explain the way he felt.

She introduced him to her mother and Kenny, and to Lynette's great relief Jack liked her brother. He wanted to spend time with Kenny so they began taking him to lunch at The Sextant on the Columbia River so Kenny could watch the boats pass. They took him to the airport to see planes taking off, to stock car races and baseball games, to the Hotcake House and to the horse track. Jack took them camping near Mount Hood. Neither she nor Kenny had ever camped before. They had never sat by a campfire. Jack was the first man that Kenny ever really liked. He was the first man Kenny ever ran to and hugged when he saw him.

There were times when Lynette was certain that Jack had been sent by her grandfather to save her life. When they would go to the Hotcake House she would secretly pray to herself and thank her grandfather for remembering her and caring enough about her to bring Jack to her. Thank you, thank you, thank you, she'd say.

★

But after a year it started, the old Lynette would reappear. In those moments her sadness and hopelessness and anger would rush past her like a speeding car. It nearly broke her when it first happened because she realized she hadn't rid herself of who she had been. She hadn't rid herself of herself, and once she knew that, it became a fog that chased her, a fog that would never completely disappear.

At first she was able to keep it in control because it only came when she was tired, sick or too drunk. Over time, though, it took more and more work. She began to have to force herself to act happy. She told Jack none of this because she was certain that if he knew how much she was struggling and what she was really like, he would leave her.

It came out first in Seaside. They had been together a year and four months when there was a beach party to celebrate Jack's brother's graduation from mechanic school. His parents were there. His aunts and uncles and cousins and grandparents. Lynette was so nervous to meet the extended family, and so nervous that they wouldn't like her, that she began to drink. Jack took her around and introduced her to everyone. His grandmother told Lynette she was the cutest girl she'd ever seen in Oregon. The old woman hugged her and wouldn't let her go. The whole family was nice to her, decent and kind, but none of it brought relief, only a building pressure she didn't know how to stop. She couldn't catch her breath. It was like she was drowning and falling at the same time.

A bonfire was started, night came, and slowly Jack's

family went home. A real party began with Jack and Henry's old high-school friends. It was summer, there were no clouds in the sky and it was warm. Someone had brought a portable stereo and people smoked weed and passed around a bottle and drank beer. Jack left her with his brother to go to the bathroom. When he came back, he talked to friends of his near the fire and then after a while he began talking to a redhead who Lynette knew had been his high-school girlfriend. They spoke only for a few minutes, but she was drunk and tired of trying so hard and terrified to be staying at his parents' house, and she threw a full beer can at him and ran down the beach into the darkness. She started crying and couldn't stop. She came to a street and then to another and made it to Highway 101, where she began walking north on the side of the road.

Jack found her an hour later sitting outside a closed Les Schwab tyre shop. He parked his truck and rushed out to her where she sat against a wall. 'I was so worried about you,' he told her, and tried to put his arms around her. 'What's going on? What did I do?'

Lynette pushed him away as hard as she could. 'Why don't you just go back and fuck your redhead. I never trusted you. I never . . . I fucking hate you and I fucking hate it here and I hate your whole stupid fucking family.'

It was the first time she'd gotten angry at him or said things like that to him, and as she did she could see his face change. Like a man watching his best friend drown. Terror and horror. He slumped down to the ground. He whispered to her, 'Why are you saying this?'

Lynette knew, even as it was happening, that she had started their ruin that night. Because she didn't tell him why. She couldn't. She said only, 'Can I get a bus back to Portland?'

He stood up sadly. 'I guess you could. Probably tomorrow, though. It's too late now. But I'll give you a ride. It's the least I can do.'

In the truck she leaned against the passenger-side window and wouldn't speak.

Jack tried to apologize, he tried to get her to talk, but she wouldn't and after a while she closed her eyes. When he stopped in front of her mother's house two hours later he was weeping. 'What did I do?' he whispered. 'I just don't understand what I did. I went out with that girl when I was a junior in high school. She's married now and has a kid. I don't like her that way . . . I just don't understand and I don't want to leave it this way. I love you more than anything and I just don't know what's going on or what I did that was so bad.'

Lynette said nothing. She got out of his truck and went into her house and down into the basement. She didn't get up to do anything but use the toilet until she had to go to work two days later.

*

A week passed and late one night she went to his apartment. He answered the door in his underwear. She broke down crying and collapsed on the ground and told him how sorry she was, how she had never been in love before and how she was insecure and jealous. She told him she didn't understand what had happened in Seaside but promised it would never happen again. She told him over and over that she loved him. She did everything she could think of to get him back.

And she did. That night he told her he loved her so much and had been so broken up over her that he hadn't been able to sleep. Sometimes at work he'd had to lock himself in the bathroom and sit down just to catch his breath, and for the first time in his life, he said, he'd felt hopeless, completely hopeless.

The next day they both called in sick and stayed in bed. She barely let him breathe. In the afternoon she got up and made them breakfast and when night came she made them dinner. It took two weeks for him to relax around her again. For a while he tried to get her to talk about that night, but always she would avoid it. She was too frightened it would come back if she did. Her answer was to give more of herself to him. She began doing his laundry and cleaning his apartment. She went wherever he wanted to go and ate whatever he wanted to eat. Jack would say things like, 'Shit, Lynette, I know you don't like eating at Santa Cruz all the time. You pick the place. Let's go where you want.' But she wouldn't. She decided to never say no to him, that she would give anything and everything to him and by doing so she would be more of him and less of her. She would try to erase herself completely.

He proposed to her six months later. He bought her a ring and found a one-bedroom house near Pier Park at the end of St Johns. By then he had become certified as a welder, made good money and could pay the rent. She was in charge of the electric and gas bills and groceries. It was the nicest house she'd ever lived in. The floors were oak and the kitchen had been remodelled. There was a dishwasher, and in the basement a washing machine and dryer. The bathroom had a shower and a separate tub. They bought house plants and second-hand furniture. They put up posters and pictures. They had a yard and she planted flowers and they talked about getting a dog. Jack made her a key to his truck and taught her how to drive. She finally got a licence. Once again it was like living in a dream that never ended.

But one morning she woke up and the darkness was back. It was all she could do to get out of bed and go to work. It became such an effort to seem happy that one night she went to a movie by herself and on the way home she closed her eyes and walked out onto Lombard Street and was nearly hit by a truck.

She began going home more to see Kenny, hoping that he would help take the darkness away, but she only ended up taking it out on her mother. She threw a bowl full of Golden Grahams and milk against a wall and screamed at her. She broke down crying on the floor, saying she wanted to die.

Thanksgiving came and they went to Jack's parents' house for dinner. She wore her engagement ring and a new dress. She brought two apple pies she'd made at the bakery. She didn't drink and she helped with the dishes. She was polite, said funny things, and Jack made sure he paid attention to her. They didn't go out drinking with his brother and their old friends. They went to bed early and he held her in his old basement room. They had sex on his high-school bed while his parents were at the store.

For Christmas they went back. A new dress, two apple-and-cranberry pies and Lynette trying harder and harder to be good. Jack's mother took her aside and told her how happy she was that Lynette was becoming a part of the family. She said she couldn't wait for the wedding, for their grandkids. When the Christmas visit ended, Lynette left Jack's parents' house so exhausted that during the truck ride home she wished she was dead. Jack held her hand as he drove. He leaned over and asked her, 'Are you okay? You seem tired . . . Is there anything I can do? Is there anything you want to talk about?'

★

There were two separate men who came into the bakery each day. Both flirted with her and asked her out, and she showed them her engagement ring, but now she began to think about them. When she had sex with Jack she thought of them. The darkness went away when she was like that. When she thought of dying or stepping in front of a car or having sex with someone else or getting shot in a robbery. It all brought relief.

Summer came and Jack's brother Henry got a job at a Ford dealership in Portland and stayed with them on their couch. She did the things she thought she was supposed to do for a visiting brother. She made dinner, she kept the house clean, she didn't flirt but she was nice. She tried to be Jack's honest and loyal girlfriend. The three of them saw movies together, they drank together and drove around in Jack's truck together, Lynette in the middle.

She read about a woman who ran every time she was depressed so she began running. Jack bought her shoes and sweats and for a while it kept the darkness at bay. When the bakery lost its assistant pastry worker, she took the job. The shift started at 4 a.m. but she loved it. She didn't have to be polite or nice or talk to customers. She got to make scones and cookies and pastries. She was able to bring comfort to people without talking to them, without giving herself to them. And for a while the new position helped.

But Henry didn't move out. He was there every night for three months. The two brothers began drinking after work together and one night Lynette woke up to them in the kitchen with a woman she'd never seen. The woman was young and pretty. She had black hair and tattoos on her arms. The kitchen table was covered with beer cans and Jack was at the stove making pancakes.

Lynette came from the bedroom in her pyjamas. 'What are you doing?' she asked, her voice already trembling.

'I'm sorry we woke you but I'm making you pancakes.' He was smiling and drunk. There was bacon frying in a pan. He had the cast-iron griddle out and a box of Krusteaz buttermilk pancake mix. 'They were going to be ready by the time you got up at three thirty.' He looked at the clock on the stove. 'It's three twenty-eight right now so pretty good timing. I even put blueberries in them because those are your favourite.'

'But who is she?' Lynette pointed to the woman.

'It's Henry's friend Roxy,' Jack said.

'Get her out of my house,' Lynette cried, her voice almost hysterical. And then it all came out of her. She threw a glass at Henry and screamed that she hated him, screamed that he was ruining their lives. She screamed at Jack that he was going to fuck the woman and then she screamed at Roxy and tried to hit her. Jack had to hold her back. She didn't know what had happened after that, but by the end she was left in the kitchen, alone, with everyone gone, the bacon burning, the smoke alarm going off and the box of pancake mix spilled out on the floor.

When she got back from work that afternoon Henry's things were gone. Jack could barely speak to her when he got home. She broke down sobbing and begged him not to leave her. She said she would do anything to make up for what she had done.

'I'm not gonna leave you,' he said. 'I'm sorry I was drunk. I was an idiot to make pancakes and stay up so late. I really am sorry for that. But that girl, Roxy, my brother likes her. I don't like her. I just met her and have nothing to do with her. And I've been trying to get my brother to leave. I have, and I've told you that. My mom said I was crazy to let him live here as long as he has. But he's my brother and he says he's been looking for a place. I don't know what to do. I've told you all this over and over. You know I have. My brother staying here so long and me being drunk and up so late is all my fault. I'll take the blame for that. But I just don't understand what happens to you. Why can't you tell me you're getting upset? Why can't we just talk about it? And the things you say are so fucking mean. They're just so awful . . . You say the meanest things I've ever heard anyone say.'

Lynette collapsed on the couch. 'I don't even know what I say when I'm like that. I swear I don't. I just know I'm sorry.' She couldn't even look at him. She moved her face against the back of the couch. 'I don't know what's wrong with me but . . . I swear I'll die if you leave me.'

'I won't leave you. Jesus, I'm not saying that.'

'I'm serious,' she whispered, full of tears. 'If you leave me, I'll kill myself.'

Jack grabbed her and hugged her. 'Please don't say that. Please don't even think about that. I'm not gonna leave. I won't ever leave you. We just need to be able to talk about it. I just need to know what to do.'

★

A week later Lynette came home from work to find Jack's mom, Tina, in their house, sitting at the kitchen table. A pot of coffee was brewing. She had taken the day off work and driven up from Seaside to talk to Lynette, but Lynette was so scared and embarrassed that she couldn't stop crying. In broken sentences she told Tina she didn't know what happened to her. She didn't mean to get so mad. It just overtook her, consumed her. She laid her head on the kitchen table. 'I try so hard to be what he wants. I try so hard to be good but I get lost.'

Tina held Lynette's hands. 'I think you need some help, hon,' she said. 'You need to talk to somebody. You might need medication, but you'll be alright. I'll help you find a counsellor.'

'But I've ruined everything.'

'You haven't ruined everything,' said Tina. 'Just tell Henry you're sorry, make him a chocolate cake and bring him a twelve-pack of beer. And look, it's not the worst thing in the world for him to be a little scared of you. Anyway, I told him he should have moved out of your place two months ago. I'd have done the same thing and, to tell you the truth, I have.'

'What about Jack?'

'Jack's different. He's madly in love with you. But he's sensitive and you've really scared him. Just give him time and get some help. If he knows you're getting help he'll start to relax again. He'll come back around.'

Tina left her with the names of two different therapists but Lynette called neither. She was too scared of the darkness to even think about it. She did, however, bring a cake and a twelve-pack of beer to Henry's new apartment and apologized.

At home she realized Jack had become different. She could tell he didn't love her the way he once had. He got home later from work. He didn't initiate sex. Where in the past he couldn't get enough of her, she now had to seduce him, and because of that she was certain he would leave her. And that made her worse. One evening she locked him out of the house when he worked late and he was forced to sleep in his truck. She tried to start fights and when they came home drunk from a concert one night she threatened to kill herself by grabbing a bottle of Tylenol PM and attempting to swallow them all in front of him. He stopped her and again broke down crying, begging her to tell him what was going on. But she couldn't. She just woke up the next morning even more certain that he would leave her, and stopped taking the pill.

★

Two months later she was pregnant. She waited another two months, until she was certain, and then decided to tell him. It was a Sunday morning. It was the only day they had off together. But when she woke up he wasn't in bed, he was in the kitchen making sandwiches. He and a coworker were going fishing.

'But we were going to spend the day together,' she said.

'I know, but this is the last time I can go fishing this year.'

'Please don't leave,' she said. 'I have something to tell you.'

'What is it?' he asked.

'I'm pregnant.'

Jack didn't go fishing that day. He just sat on the couch in a daze. He didn't say anything. He didn't ask her how she could be pregnant when she was on the pill. He didn't call his parents and tell them the good news. They didn't stop by his brother's apartment to celebrate. He just sat there and then after a while he got up and left the house and she went back to bed and sobbed. He didn't come back for two days and when he did it was with Henry and all three of them sat at the kitchen table.

'I know it's weird that my brother's here,' said Jack. He was pale and there were dark circles around his eyes and she noticed for the first time that he'd lost weight. He looked sick. 'But the truth is . . . well . . . I'm scared of you. It kills me to say it because I loved you so much, but it's true. I really am scared of you . . . And I can't marry someone or have a kid with someone I'm scared of. So now I'm . . .' He glanced at his brother and then his voice lowered and he looked at the table when he spoke. 'If you want to have the kid that's your right, but if you have it I'm gonna fight for custody. I talked to my folks and we'll raise the baby in Seaside. I think it's the best thing for the kid. I don't mean to be cruel, I'm not saying this to be cruel, but I don't think you're fit to be a mother. You're a good person a lot of the time but you're also a really mean person. You have mental problems that you don't seem to want to fix . . . I just don't understand what happens to you and you don't seem to want or be able to let me understand. You won't even try getting help. No kid needs to get in the middle of that. No kid needs to get yelled at the way you yell . . . I want you to know I really did love you and I haven't ever been in love before. But now, for the first time in my life, I feel depressed, depressed all the time. I just wake up every day feeling horrible.' He stopped and looked up at her. 'Jesus, I wish you a lot of luck in life, I really do, and I'll always miss you and care about you, but I'm moving out. I'm leaving when we get done talking. I'll pay rent for two months but I can't afford any more after that. I'm sorry but I just can't. I gotta find a new place to live and all that . . . And let me know what you want to do about this place. I called the landlord and told him what's happening. He'll put the house in your name if you want. I don't care about the deposit or the furniture or any of the stuff we bought together. It's yours . . . I guess that's it. Henry and I are gonna move my stuff out now.' He paused. 'And I'm just gonna say this too, just to be clear. I'm not here to discuss any of it. It's too late for that. I'm just leaving. I know we'll need to stay in contact about the baby. I'd prefer it by text or email. I'll help in any way I can if you decide to have it. I'll give you money, as much money as I can each month until then. But after that I think it's best if me and my family raise it and we'll all fight with everything we have to make sure that happens.'

Lynette didn't say anything. She put her head on the kitchen table and closed her eyes, and Henry and Jack moved out his things. When his truck was loaded he set his house key on the kitchen table and they drove away and Lynette went to bed.

She lost her job. For a month she stayed in the house and then abandoned it, taking only her clothes, and moved back to her mother's basement, completely broke. Two weeks after that she called JJ, who she hadn't spoken to in five years, and he took her to an abortion clinic, paid for it and let her recover at his house. A week later she took the bus to Jack's work and waited until he was on lunch break. She was haggard and thin and walked slowly to where he sat leaning against the building, eating a sack lunch.

'I hope you'll forgive me someday,' she whispered. 'But I did it . . . We don't have a baby any more. You don't have to worry about it or me ever again. I just want you to know I'm sorry you met me. I really am sorry for that.'

He looked at her and tears welled in his eyes but he said nothing and Lynette walked back to her house, blacked out the windows in the basement and gave up. Days passed where she would only get out of bed to use the toilet. She lost nearly fifteen pounds and two separate times she had a box cutter in her hand to kill herself, but each time she couldn't do it. It wasn't the memory of before, the blood on the bed, that stopped her, it was only the thought of her mother's screams and Kenny's panic that kept her from doing it. She had caused so much wreckage in her short life that she knew she couldn't cause even more.

A month passed, and then one day her mother came home from work and sat in a fold-out chair across from Lynette. 'I'm gonna tell you the way it is and see what you want to do. Two months ago Cheryl cut my hours to thirty and I haven't been able to pay our bills on that. When you were living with Jack I struggled to keep up with them but I could do it if I used my credit card when I got short. But now, with my hours cut, I can't. I just don't have enough money. I didn't tell you any of this 'cause you were in love and I was happy you had found someone. Happy that you were finally free to be you . . . But now . . . well, here it is, Lynette. I'm gonna lose the house if you don't get a job. I've already used all my savings. I told Mr Claremont our situation and he said he'd give us a free month to get back on our feet but that was all he could do. I maxed out my credit card to pay the electric and gas bill. We have no grocery money. I called my aunt in Yakima and asked for a loan but all she would give us is a hundred dollars. A lousy hundred dollars and I don't know when she's gonna mail it or if she really will. Your father won't return any of my calls. I've tried a dozen times and not once has he picked up or called back, even when I left a message explaining the situation. Marsha's not charging me anything right now for taking care of Kenny, but that won't last forever. I've run out of things to sell and I've almost asked Cheryl for a loan and as you know that would be a really hard thing for me to do. So that's where I am. I'm at the bottom and about ready to give up. So if you care about me at all or about what will happen to Kenny if I do fall apart then you'll get up and get your shit together. Ask for help and I'll get you help. Ask to go to a doctor and I'll get you to a doctor. If you want me to run over Jack I will. I'll find out where he lives and I'll beat him, I'll kill the piece of shit for hurting you. I'll do anything you want but we have to do something. Because we're tied to you, Lynette. Kenny and I are hooked onto you and you're like an anchor and you just keep going down and we can't go down any more without losing everything. So I'm on my knees. I really am begging. Ask for help and get better or destroy us. It's your choice.'

Lynette said nothing. She waited until her mother went upstairs and then for the first time in six days she showered. She washed her sheets and her pyjamas. She was weak and tired but she helped her mother cook dinner. It took her four days to get the strength to leave the house but she did. She took a bus to the Tulip Pastry Shop and begged for her job back.

★

It was two years ago that she'd seen Henry again at the St Johns Parade. She and Kenny were standing in front of the movie theatre watching the makeshift floats and the old cars pass when Henry walked by with two other men. He saw her and stopped, and she couldn't help herself and asked about Jack.

Henry told her his brother had left Portland two weeks after he'd heard the news about the baby. He'd gone back to Seaside. 'He was so messed up he moved in with our folks and saw a head doctor. He was there for a year or so. Then he got a job as welder in Bend. He bought a house and got a puppy. He took the dog to get its shots and met his wife, who's a vet. They've got a kid now. He's doing really good, he's happy. But, man oh man, you fucked him up for a while. Never seen him so laid out . . . He's good now, though . . . But I will say this. You know that easy-going thing he had? You know that way he was?'

'Yeah,' Lynette said.

'He doesn't have that any more.'

17

It was 5.50 a.m. when Lynette finished her third cup of coffee and left the truck stop. It took seven tries for the car to start, and she drove to Columbia Boulevard and into the industrial section of town. At 42nd she turned north and a dead-end sign appeared. All the businesses on the street were closed; she passed a mechanic shop, a warehouse and a paved lot filled with semi-trailers. At the street's end, on the right, was a sanitation company with rows of green Sani-Huts, and on the left was a twelve-foot-high chain-link fence topped with razor wire encircling a two-acre lot with more than forty cars and trucks inside. The vehicles looked new: BMWs, Audis, Mercedes and Cadillacs as well as Ford, Chevy and Dodge pickup trucks. Toward the back of the lot was a trailer home. The windows were lit but curtains covered them. The chain-link front gate had a plastic sign attached to it that read *Hawk's Auto Service and Sales*.

Lynette stopped and got out of the car. She opened the trunk and underneath the spare tyre placed the money she had gotten from Cody, next to the money and the other things from the safe. A green plastic toolbox was in the back corner and she opened it. Inside was twenty dollars, two flares, a screwdriver, a wrench and a can of Mace. She put the Mace in her right coat pocket and had the Buck knife in her left. An old Burgerville bag was under the jumper cables, and she emptied it and put the cocaine inside. After that she set her purse in the trunk, locked it, got back in the car and pulled up to the front gate. Two spotlights hung from a telephone pole and shone down. There was no intercom. She honked the car's horn, a minute passed, then the gate opened and she drove in.

The trailer had a large gravel parking lot in front of it and she turned the car around, facing the now-closed gate, and shut off the engine. She carried the fast-food bag up metal porch steps to the front door and knocked.

The man who answered was in his late forties. He was short and bald and dressed in Kelly green pants with a white T-shirt tucked into them. He was as defined and muscle-bound as a bodybuilder.

'Lynette?' he said in a friendly voice.

She nodded.

He smiled and backed away from the door. 'I'm Rodney. Come on in.'

'I don't feel comfortable going inside,' she told him nervously. 'Can we just do it out here?'

The man shook his head. 'Sorry, I can't do that. I don't know if any of my neighbours will be watching or showing up. It's early but still, you never know. It would look funny. So come on in. I swear nothing bad will happen. But if you can't, I see you turned your car around already. To get out all you do is drive to the gate and it'll open automatically.'

Behind the man Lynette saw an ironing board with a shirt on it and a grey cat sitting on the kitchen table. A set of golf clubs was leaned against it. The TV was on – she couldn't see it but she could hear Rhonda Shelby giving the weather report. It was Rhonda's voice and the cat on the table that made her think it would be safe enough to go inside.

'If you show me you have the money then I'll come in. But I won't come in unless you do that.'

'Give me a second to finish ironing, then,' he said, and shut the door. He didn't open it again for five minutes. The rain soaked her face and hair. Her feet were numb. When he opened the door he was wearing a pink golf shirt tucked into the Kelly green pants. He showed her a roll of money with a rubber band around it. 'There's more than three grand here,' he said. 'I just have to count it out.'

'Okay,' she said.

He opened the door wider and she went inside.

The floor of the trailer was linoleum. To the left of the door was an office area with a large wooden desk. Behind it was a leather chair and a long bookcase with stacks of papers, books and old mechanic manuals. On the wood-panelled walls were posters of golfers and framed maps and aerial pictures of golf courses.

To the right of the door was the kitchen. The appliances and counter were white and the cabinets were laminated pine. The living room had a yellow vinyl couch, a TV, a bench press, free weights and a rack that held six dumb-bells of different weights. She turned back to the kitchen. The ironing board was gone and the cat was no longer on the table. The trailer looked like it had just been cleaned. She could smell Pine-Sol and coffee. Rodney stood in front of a toaster and put in eight frozen French Toaster Sticks.

'You want some breakfast?'

'No, that's okay,' said Lynette.

'Don't be so nervous,' he said. 'And please take off your shoes.'

She shook her head and whispered, 'I'm not gonna take off my shoes.'

'Then don't move and I'll get a towel,' he said, and briefly looked at her. It was then that she saw a flash of anger. She'd made a mistake coming inside. He went past the living room and down a hall, then came back with a turquoise bath towel and spread it out on the floor. 'Stand on this. I spend a lot of time trying to keep this place clean. The least you could do is respect that.'

She stepped on the towel.

'I was just getting up when JJ texted. It was a strange call to get that early.'

'How do you know JJ?' she asked.

'When we were kids my brother was in a band that practised at JJ's house. I used to hang out there. You know the place?'

'Yeah,' she said.

The French Toaster Sticks popped up and he pushed them down again. A brown belt sat on the kitchen table and he put it on. He hooked a leather cell-phone case and a pocketknife to it and drank a glass of water. The sticks popped up again and he took them out and buttered them. He grabbed a plastic bottle of Log Cabin syrup from a cabinet, covered the toaster sticks with it and put the bottle back. He opened a drawer, took out a fork, sat down at the table and began eating.

'Is it snowing out?'

'No,' she said, 'just raining.'

'They said it might flurry. I'm playing golf in an hour. I went out two hundred and seventy-five times last year. Only got snowed out once. You're gonna have to wait for me to finish eating. I hate doing coke on an empty stomach and I'm not buying it without trying it. Where did you get it, anyway?'

'A friend of mine gave it to me.'

'Just gave you a half a kilo?'

'Yeah.'

'Who's your friend?'

'A girl I know. She owed me some money and couldn't pay me so she gave me the coke instead.'

'Where did she get it?'

'I don't know anything about that. She just gave it to me and I don't do it myself.'

'Why the rush on selling it?'

'I just don't like having it with me. It makes me nervous. So I called JJ. I used to be friends with him and I knew he would know what to do. I explained it to him and he called you. I just want to get rid of it.'

'In the middle of the night you decided all this.'

'I guess.'

Rodney got up, refilled his glass with water, sat back down and kept eating.

Lynette again looked around the room. 'What kind of work do you do?'

'I repossess cars,' he said. 'The ones out there on the lot are in the process of going back to the dealers they were bought from.'

'All those cars have been repossessed?'

'All except mine. You'd be surprised how many people don't own their cars outright.' He paused and finished the French toast, then pushed the plate away from him and licked his lips. 'One thing you find out in my line of work is that most people act like they have more than they really do. That they're better off than they really are. It's always the same kind of people too. I've been doing this for over twenty-five years and it never changes. Rednecks and gangsters want to be rich but most of them aren't rich. Rednecks with their trucks and gangsters with their SUVs and Cadillacs. And on the other side are the full-of-shit people trying to act white-collar rich by driving BMWs and Mercedes and Audis.'

He got up, put the dish in the sink and started the faucet. He washed the plate, the fork and knife, and set them on a wooden rack to the left of the sink. 'I don't mind the white-collar ones but the rednecks and the gangsters try to kill you when you repo their rig. Here they are driving trucks they can't afford, skipping out on payments, and then they try to kill you for calling them on it. They signed the deal – has nothing to do with me. I'm only the result of them not paying their bill. But still they try to kill me when I'm only following the law. The white-collar wannabes just cry and whine and tell me they're gonna sue me. I'll be out in Beaverton, Hillsdale or Tigard and some asshole will be yelling in the middle of the street. "You can't do this to me. I'll get my lawyer and he'll sue you. When I'm done you'll be in prison!" It's all bullshit. You never hear from them again unless they buy another car they can't afford and then of course the same thing happens again. Over and over. You know, I've never had one person say, "I'm sorry I fucked up and I bought this car and I can't pay for it. It's my fault. Here are the keys. Can I please get my CDs and the baby seat out?" Nowadays people buy things they can't afford just 'cause they're able to and then when it hits the fan they blame the people selling the stuff.' He laughed. 'I've begun to hate people that don't pay what they're supposed to pay. That don't honour their side of the deal. After all these years it's really starting to make me sick. You get a bill, you pay the bill. It's pretty simple. You want to buy something, then save for it, have some fucking patience. Pay for it with cash. It used to be like that in this country. Now no one wants to wait. No one wants to save for what they want. Credit cards and credit cards and credit cards. People getting things they haven't earned, that they haven't sweated for. Half the time they're buying things they didn't even know they wanted. And let me tell you, getting things you haven't earned does nobody any good. How can it be good that the second you want something you can get it? Go online and hit a button and then you own it. But really you don't own it and when the payment's due you're about eight miles from remembering you even wanted the thing in the first place. So then you just stick your head in the sand or cry or throw a tantrum. Or if you're a real piece of shit you come out with a gun and try to kill me for a bill you haven't paid in six months. They'd rather kill a guy than take a bus. They'd rather kill a guy than drive a piece-of-shit beater like what you got out there. What is it, a Sentra?'

'Yeah,' said Lynette.

'Nineteen ninety-three?'

'Ninety-two.'

'I had a red ninety-four when I was in college. They aren't bad cars for running around town. Do you want a cup of coffee?'

'No.'

'I'm just gonna get a splash more,' he said, and got up again. There was an old Black & Decker coffee machine in the corner of the kitchen. He filled his cup and poured powdered creamer into it, stirred it with a fork and sat down again. 'I just don't get it. For example, my cousin works construction. He's always just been one of the grunts, never moved up, never tried to be a foreman or a lead. Not sure why he's never tried, but he hasn't. About twenty years ago he got married and together he and his wife squeaked out a loan on a hundred-thousand-dollar house. This was in 2000 or 2001. The house was a piece of shit but that's where he was at. That's what he could afford. His wife worked at Target, they had a kid, and like I said he worked construction. You know where Chinese Village is?'

'Sure,' said Lynette. 'They just tore it down.'

He nodded. 'They had a house right by it, off 82nd and Washington. A fucked-up busy street and a small house. I didn't like the place but it made sense to me 'cause that's what the guy deserved. That's what they could afford. Five or six years go by and in the mail they start getting these offers. He starts getting pre-approved home loans for three hundred and fifty thousand dollars. Now what the fuck's going on there? Nothing's changed. He's got the same old job and, sure, his wife doesn't work at Target any more, no, she works at Bed Bath & Beyond. Same hours, almost part-time, almost full-time, around the same pay. So why the fuck would they get pre-approved like that? Just out of the blue when a few years before they were busting his balls about a hundred-thousand-dollar loan. Makes no sense, right? Anyway, he won't listen to me. His wife of course wants a nicer house for their kid, he wants a nicer house 'cause he's sick of living on a busy street. He'd always tell me, "The traffic, man, it drives me crazy. And all those weird fuckers on 82nd always walk by." I told him to get double-paned windows and plant a hedge or put up a fence. A hell of a lot cheaper. But does he listen to me? No, of course not. He buys a place in Happy Valley for three-thirty and of course they have to buy new furniture to go into their new house and, well, you know what happened?'

'No, what happened?'

'He lost the house and he and his wife split up and now he's renting an apartment from me. I own a six-unit complex on Dekum, by Woodlawn Park. You know that area?'

'A little,' she said.

'Well, he can barely scrape together rent on the discounted friends-and-family price I gave him because they've garnished his wages over child support. I have him managing the place now because he's late on rent almost every month. It's the only way I can justify not kicking him out. He's a fucking idiot and he ain't gonna get out from

under it 'cause he's getting old and he's still working construction, still a grunt, but now of course he's getting tired.
His back is fucked up, his knees are fucked. If he would
have just accepted the shitty house on 82nd he'd probably
own it outright by now. He'd probably still be married. But
I guess that's just human nature. Anyway, I've eaten, so
where is it?'

Lynette kept her feet on the turquoise bath towel and
took the package out of the Burgerville bag, set it on the
kitchen table and pushed it toward him.

From his pants pocket he took out a charcoal-coloured
vial and opened it. The lid had a small thin spoon connected to it and he dipped it into the cocaine, put the
spoon to his nose and snorted it. He did it twice in each
nostril. His eyes watered and his face grew red. He looked
at her and let out a quick intense breath. 'Where did your
friend get this?'

'I don't know.'

'Well, it's good.'

'Then it's a deal? JJ said three thousand dollars. He
said that was good for you. It's good for me too.'

His face grew redder, like something was wrong with
him, and then he just lifted his right hand and pointed to
the door. 'The deal is you can get out of my trailer now.'

'What do you mean?' asked Lynette.

'JJ says you owe him money and the thing is, JJ owes
me money. Has for a few years. I'd be more pissed at him
but I've known him for a long time and he was nice to my
brother. My brother died in a motorcycle accident and JJ
bought two kegs for the funeral. He helped cater it. He

was really upset and he was about the only one outside me and my parents who really was. Maybe that's why I've let him slide on what he owes me. But now, with this, he can pay me back. That's what we both decided. You owe him, he owes me. You give me the coke and JJ and me are even. And you'll be even with JJ too.'

'But I don't owe JJ any money,' Lynette said. 'He's lying about that. I paid back what I owed him years ago. He helped me out once but I paid him. I put the money in an envelope and put it in his mailbox and then I called him to make sure he got it and he said he did. I swear to God. And that was over seven years ago. Except for tonight, I haven't seen him since back then. He's lying.'

Rodney smiled and when he did she could see his teeth were unnaturally white and perfectly straight. They were dentures. 'He told me you'd say that. He also said you were crazy. That you have mental problems and to watch out. He said a lot of things about you. Anyway, I've known him for twenty years, and you I don't know at all. So I have to trust him more than you. So I'll let you leave right now and everything will be okay. Just take your piece-of-shit car and get out of my lot.'

Lynette reached for the cocaine but Rodney exploded out of his chair and with both hands hit her so hard in the chest that she flew back into a waist-high table near the front door. A glass lamp on the table crashed to the ground and she fell back on it. Shards of glass cut into her back and stuck there, and she struggled to stand up. When she did, Rodney had a stainless-steel revolver pointed at her.

'You're leaving right now.'

'I don't understand why you're doing this,' she said with effort. 'I don't owe JJ anything.'

'JJ said you're a piece of shit and you owe him money. I knew just looking at you that you'd bitch and lie and waste my time and I'm playing golf in less than an hour. So leave, and if you do, your debt to JJ is done and his debt to me is done and you won't be a piece of shit any more. At least where this is concerned.'

Lynette slowly walked toward the table. 'But like I said, I don't owe him anything. If you know him at all you know he's a liar. Just give me the three thousand we agreed on and I'll leave. Give me the money or the cocaine. You say you're honest. If you are you'll do the right thing.'

Rodney set the gun on the kitchen table and took the roll of money from his pocket. 'I'll give you a couple hundred bucks but then I want you to get the fuck out of here or I'll force you out and you won't like that.'

He looked down to take the rubber band off the roll and when he did Lynette grabbed the Mace from her pocket and shot it at his face. It hit him in the eyes and mouth and he dropped the money on the table and doubled over screaming. He reached for the gun but couldn't find it. Lynette grabbed it and the money and put them in her coat pocket. Rodney was coughing and began throwing up on the floor as he stumbled out of the room toward the back hallway. Lynette pulled her scarf around her nose and mouth. Her eyes were watering and she had trouble seeing but she followed after him and continued to spray his head until he locked himself inside the bathroom.

18

Her car started on the fourth try. Lynette could hardly see and her coughing wouldn't stop but she drove to the gate and it opened just like Rodney had said. She pulled out and made it to Columbia Boulevard and headed west. The windshield was little more than a blur with her eyes watering and the rain falling. She drove under twenty miles an hour, in pain and hunched over the steering wheel.

After a mile she made it to a McDonald's parking lot and turned off the engine. She put Rodney's money in her pants pocket and his gun under her front seat and got out. In the parking lot she took off her scarf and Mace-ruined coat, which was pulling on the glass stuck in her back. She rolled them both into a ball, dropped them in a nearby trash can and went inside.

The bathroom was empty and she washed her hands and face, her neck and arms a half-dozen times, then dunked her head under the sink and washed her hair with hand soap. She dried it with paper towels and then looked at her back. Blood covered her shirt and she could feel shards of glass inside her. She went into a stall, used the toilet and counted Rodney's money. Thirty-nine hundred dollars. She put it back in her pants pocket and left.

★

It was seven in the morning when she came to her house and the white Toyota Avalon in the carport. She opened the front door and saw her mother on the couch in her orange bathrobe, the electric blanket around her, watching TV and smoking a cigarette. In front of her was a Domino's pizza box and a half-empty litre of Pepsi.

She looked at Lynette and sighed. 'Jesus, I was worried about you.'

'I was gonna call but I didn't have time, and then it was too late.' Lynette went to the thermostat and turned up the heat on the furnace. 'I want to talk but I need your help first. I got into some trouble and there's glass in my back. Can you help me get it out?'

'Glass in your back? Jesus, what happened?'

'I just panicked and tried to get all the money that was owed me. I made a lot of mistakes and got greedy. Will you meet me in the bathroom?'

Her mother nodded, got up from the couch and followed her down the hallway. Lynette turned on the bathroom light and her mother came in and saw her blood-soaked shirt.

'My God,' she said. 'Can you take it off?'

'I think so,' said Lynette, unbuttoning her shirt and crying out in pain as she pulled it off her back.

'That bad, huh?'

'Yeah.'

'You still have your fifth of Jägermeister in the freezer. Do you want me to get you a glass?'

'Maybe I better.'

'I'll get some dish towels too. I know we have hydrogen

peroxide and rubbing alcohol in the medicine cabinet. Do we have tweezers?'

'I have them downstairs in the cigar box on my dresser.'

Her mother left and Lynette sat down on the toilet seat. In the next room she could hear Kenny snoring. Finally heat started coming through the bathroom vent and she began to relax. Her mother came back wearing reading glasses and set a stack of dish towels on the sink. She handed Lynette the Jägermeister.

'God, your back is really gross-looking,' her mother said. 'There's four or five shards that I can see. You'll have to take off your bra.'

'Can you do it for me?' Lynette asked, and stood back up. 'I think I hurt my ribs too. I don't think I can move my arms back.'

Her mother unclasped the bra and helped Lynette take it off.

'Where did you get such an expensive bra?' she said, setting it on the edge of the bathtub.

'I don't really remember,' Lynette whispered, and sat back down.

'I never had a bra like that.' Her mother opened the medicine cabinet and took out a bottle of hydrogen peroxide. 'But my tits used to be as good as yours. Maybe even better, but of course then came two kids. Jesus, wait until you get to my age, until you can't lose weight and your tits sag.'

Lynette took a drink from the glass. She sat hunched over on the toilet seat, her arms resting on her legs. Her mother sat on the edge of the bathtub next to her.

'What did you get yourself into?'

'I'll tell you later,' said Lynette. 'Do you have enough light?'

'I think so,' said her mother. 'I'll get the big pieces first. After that I'll rinse the cuts out with hydrogen peroxide and then maybe I'll get the flashlight and look again. Do you remember where the flashlight is?'

'It should be in the desk by the front door. If not, it's in Kenny's room.'

'You should take another drink 'cause I'm getting ready to pull them out.'

Lynette had another sip and set the glass on the floor. 'I'm ready.'

'I don't want to hurt you,' her mother said.

'It's okay. I know it's going to hurt.'

Her mother began with the tweezers, pulling out the pieces of glass and dropping them in the sink. Lynette cried out and tears filled her eyes.

'These tweezers don't grip very good but I think I got most of them,' her mother said, and stopped. 'I'm going to get the flashlight now to make sure.' She left the room and came back with a red plastic flashlight and an old shirt. She found two more smaller pieces in Lynette's lower back and then rinsed each cut out with hydrogen peroxide. After that she put Neosporin over the cuts and covered three of them with Band-Aids. The two larger wounds she covered with gauze held to Lynette's back with masking tape. 'The big ones might need stitches. I don't know. They're not really bleeding now. Maybe we can look online and see what to do.'

'Alright,' Lynette said.

'Jesus, I was worried about you.'

'I'm sorry.'

'I'm just glad you're okay. I brought my button-down paint shirt we used when we painted the kitchen. It's clean and you can get blood on it and it won't make a difference.'

'Thanks,' Lynette said, and stood up. Her mother helped her put the shirt on.

They went back to the living room. Her mother got a glass of chocolate milk from the fridge and sat down on the couch. Lynette sat in the wooden chair near the door and took another drink of Jägermeister.

'Where were you last night?' her mother asked.

'Nowhere, really . . . I am sorry I didn't call. I know it must have made you worried. Are you going to work today?'

She shook her head. 'I didn't sleep last night. I already called in. You get any sleep at all?'

'No,' said Lynette. 'But I'm okay. Look, I've been thinking a lot since we talked yesterday, trying to figure things out. I want to say first that I know I haven't been easy. I've tried to apologize as much as I can. Maybe you're right, maybe apologies don't make up for the way I was. But I've worked hard on myself. After Jack I really did struggle. You, more than anybody, know that. What I didn't tell you was that I went to a therapist twice a week for over a year, but I had to pay for it. The free place had a long waiting list and I was recommended to a different therapist and she was really good but expensive. I didn't tell you because I was spending so much money on it. I was scared you'd think I was stupid because I put all that on my credit card. I paid a lot of our bills on my credit card too, because as you know I couldn't work full-time until I got stronger. All of that's my fault . . . And I want you to hear me apologize one more time and I hope you'll accept it. I really am sorry for being so difficult. For a lot of years the only way I used to know how to get control of my life was to get mad. It was the only way I knew how to stand up for myself. I'm not making excuses, I'm just saying I'm sorry. I know that was difficult to be around. And I know it hasn't been easy between us. That's your fault and my fault and us just being who we are, living together. Mother and daughter . . . And then there's Kenny, and we both know he takes a lot out of us. I guess we've been connected a lot longer than most mothers and daughters because of him. That's hard in itself. I think it's right to say we both love him and have tried our best for him. Maybe you think my best isn't that good, maybe it isn't, but I've always tried as hard as I could. And one other thing came to me last night that I wanted to thank you for.

'I want to thank you for letting me be with Jack. I know it was hard on you, having to pay for everything on your own, and I didn't help with Kenny the way I should have when I moved in with Jack. I've never thanked you for that. For a while that was the nicest time in my life. So I just wanted you to know . . . If I get angry now, it's just because I want to help us and I get frustrated. But I've controlled my anger and my depression and each year I've gotten better. I know I have. And I hope you've seen it. You've

165

had to – at least a little, I hope . . . And one more thing I want to say. I want you to know that I appreciate all the nice things you've done for me and Kenny. You've sacrificed a lot. Maybe I haven't thanked you enough for that. But I am now. Thank you for all you've done for me, for when I came home after running away and then again after Jack. I know I have a hard time telling you about things. I think I just get so ashamed. I've been so ashamed of myself for so long that it's just hard to talk about, to admit that to you. So I'm also sorry that I couldn't explain myself better . . . I don't want to leave us. It's the last thing I want. I don't do well alone. I know that. I always fall apart when I'm alone. All I'm saying is please, please, listen. Buying this place is the first lucky break we've had in a long time. I know you don't believe it, but it's the truth. Rents keep going up and Mr Claremont's basically giving us twenty thousand dollars by selling it to us as cheap as he is. Think about how much money he's giving us by selling it to us at that price. That's luck . . . Finally, after all these years we get some luck. This house will give us something to work on, something of our own to be proud of. This city is changing so much, so fast, that I don't know what to think. It just makes me scared. I drove around last night and there are neighbourhoods I don't even recognize any more. There are streets I went to as a kid that don't look anything like they did. Division Street is like a different city. Belmont, Mississippi, Alberta, Williams, Interstate . . . You know how Kenny counts cranes?'

'He loves cranes,' her mother said, and took a drink of chocolate milk.

'There are eleven downtown. Eleven new buildings and that's just right now. He counted sixteen last summer. We're gonna get pushed out if we don't buy. That's a fact. Maybe we'll get lucky and find a decent rental but most likely we'll have to leave this neighbourhood or pay a lot more. But if we buy this place we can be in charge for once. We'll have some say. I know you think of it as just being in debt. That's not exactly true. Paying rent, we never get anything. With this we will. So I'm begging you. I'm really, really begging you with everything I have. Can we please buy this place?'

She stopped for a moment and waited for her mother to respond, but when she didn't Lynette kept going. 'Last night, why I was gone was because I was trying to get all the money I could that was owed to me, so you wouldn't have to have as big of a loan. So you wouldn't feel so handcuffed by a loan . . . I got greedy and I panicked, but I'm okay. I just wanted to bring as much money as I could. I'm not sure exactly but I think I have almost a hundred thousand dollars now. And I'll try and see if I can get a loan. Maybe they'll give me a fifty-thousand-dollar loan and if they do then we'll be partners. Equal partners. That means it's not all on you. It's on us together, exactly the same.

'And I'll do whatever I can to get you another car or to figure out how to get a loan and keep your new car. There are so many different ways we can make this work. I just wasn't thinking about all the possibilities. I wasn't being smart. And we really can make this place great if we try. I know we can and I have so many good plans and ideas on how to do it. But I'll need you to be onboard. I'll need you to help and be behind it. So please, please, please, let's do it.'

Lynette stopped and looked at her mother but when she did her mother turned her eyes to the TV. She held on to her cigarette and ash fell on the blanket and she left it there. 'I'm too tired to talk about this again,' she said.

'I know. I'm tired too. We're both exhausted. But we have to figure it out.'

Her mother's voice lowered until it was barely audible. 'I told you what I thought yesterday. I don't want to again. I'm sorry but I meant what I said.'

Lynette nodded, took a deep breath and exhaled. 'Okay, okay . . . I was thinking about something else last night. Maybe you're right. Maybe we need to find a different place. This house does have a lot of bad memories. Maybe too many tough times to get over. We could find a place further out, not in this neighbourhood but out in Gresham or Clackamas or Milwaukie. There's gotta be a house out there that we can afford, and I don't mind commuting if you don't.'

Her mother began to fidget but kept her eyes on the TV. Her face was grey and bloated and her lips were chapped and there was tomato sauce on her chin. 'We'll just end up in another version of this house and I don't want to commute.'

'Even in your new car?'

'You sure can be nice when you want something.'

'I want to be nice because I want to be better. I want to be the kind of person who is nice.'

Her mother looked at her cigarette, leaned over and

knocked the ash from it onto the pizza box. 'I'm exhausted and I was so worried about you I couldn't even sleep and now I can't work. I'm beat and I know this is going to upset you, but Christ, for once I have to put myself first. I don't want the loan and I don't want this house. I don't know how many times I have to tell you.'

Lynette slumped forward in the chair. She put her elbows on her knees and took another sip of her drink. 'I'm not that smart but I think I'm beginning to figure out what you're doing . . . You don't want to live with me, do you? This is about me. That's what's going on?'

Her mother picked up her glass of chocolate milk, finished it, but said nothing.

'At least say it,' Lynette whispered. 'At least let me hear it so I know it's real.'

Her mother took a long pull from her cigarette, exhaled the smoke and looked at her. 'I'm sorry, Lynette, but I don't want to live with you. I love you, I do, but I'm tired of living with you. I'm tired of being around you.'

Tears leaked down Lynette's face and she nodded. They sat for nearly five minutes in silence. The TV played and her mother stared at it.

Lynette wiped her eyes. 'Okay . . . Do you really want me to take Kenny?'

Her mother half-nodded. 'I was so upset last night I gave him a pill and packed most of his things. If you want him, take him.'

'Where are we supposed to go?'

Her mother let out an exasperated laugh. 'You're the one who said you were leaving this morning if I didn't do what you wanted. I don't know where you're supposed to go. I barely know where I'm gonna go.'

'Alright . . . Alright,' Lynette said quietly, and sighed. 'I'm gonna get out of here in a day or two. My ribs hurt and I'll have to get rid of a lot of stuff so I don't know how long it'll take, but now I don't want to stay here any more either. So I'll be fast. I'll clean out the basement and the garage and Kenny's room. You'll have to do the rest but most of this stuff is yours anyway. I'll give you an extra month's rent and bill money.' She stood up. 'I'm gonna try and sleep for a few hours.'

Her mother put out her cigarette on the pizza box. 'I'll look at your bandages when you wake up. Try not to sleep on your back.'

'Alright,' said Lynette. She went to the thermostat and turned the heat back down on the furnace, then went down to the basement. She left her clothes on, got in bed, lay on her side and collapsed into sleep.

19

The two small basement windows showed a dark-grey sky and a steady rain falling. Kenny was standing in his Superman T-shirt and pyjama bottoms with his hands around Lynette's ankle, pulling her from the bed.

'Leave me alone,' Lynette cried, and pulled the covers over her head. But Kenny wouldn't let go and after a minute she glanced at the clock: 9 a.m. She sat up in bed and looked at him. 'I'll get up, but only on one condition. You brush your teeth and put on your clothes. I'll make us breakfast after that, alright?'

Kenny smiled.

Lynette pointed her finger at him. 'I'm serious. You go upstairs and put on your red sweats. I put them on top of your dresser with your red socks. And brush your teeth for three minutes. I'll know if you don't do it that long. That's an order or I'll start counting, okay?'

Kenny made for the stairs and Lynette slowly got up from the bed. Her chest was so sore she could barely lift her arms above her head. She took off her mother's old paint shirt to see that the bandages had leaked through and onto her sheets. She put the shirt back on and went upstairs. The carport was empty. In the kitchen she made coffee and checked her phone. There were six messages from Gloria, one from JJ and one from the bakery. She deleted them all without listening. She called AT&T and told them she wanted her number changed and unlisted. They gave her a new number, she wrote it down and hung up.

She drank coffee and tried to think. JJ had never known where she lived but Gloria had been over to her house a half-dozen times. There was nothing she could do about that. And what about Rodney? She paced the room and then called three junk removal services before finding one that could do a pick-up that day at 1 p.m. After that she went to the bathroom, took off her shirt and stood in front of the mirror. Dark-purple bruising covered her chest from getting pushed by Rodney. Her breasts were swollen and sore, the left one discoloured with yellow and purple bruising. The two gauze bandages on her back were soaked in blood but the smaller ones covered in Band-Aids had no signs of blood. She took three ibuprofen, brushed her teeth and washed her face.

In the living room she turned up the heat, put an *Aladdin* DVD on the TV and set Kenny on the couch with a peanut-butter-and-jam sandwich. When he was settled she went down to the basement and began packing. Most of her clothes she put in a pile for Goodwill and packed only the best of them in the one suitcase her family had. Her other things – CDs and books and shoes she didn't wear any more – she put in her car to drop off. She stripped the sheets from both her and Kenny's beds and put them in the washer. The plastic liner covering his twin bed she took off and put in the carport. His mattress was ten years old and stained from years of urine, and she dragged it out there as well. Her mattress had once been her mother's and was ancient too. She'd have the junk men come down to the basement and take it out. Both of their second-hand dressers she broke apart and left outside. A pile formed. Everything she couldn't give away or fit in her car she put in the carport: a broken plastic dollhouse her father had given her, a bowling ball with a chip out of it, an old red backpack with a missing strap, a Coleman lantern that was in three pieces, old fishing poles, a box of cassette tapes, discarded framed posters of Superman, two chairs with broken legs and an old salon-style hairdryer on a stand that her grandmother had left them.

Her mother had packed Kenny's duffel bag with all his clothes. His TV and DVD player and his movies were also in a pile near the front door. In a cardboard box Lynette packed enough plates, forks, spoons and knives for them to get by. She then locked Kenny inside the house and made three trips to Goodwill. By the time the junk truck arrived at one she was throwing more and more things onto the pile: an old popcorn machine they'd never used, a blender that needed a screwdriver to turn on, two small lamps that had been glued back together and an end table that had a two-by-four as one of the legs. Kenny's room became empty, as did the basement.

While the two junk men loaded their truck, Lynette moved to the garage. She pulled out a kiddie pool, a metal Christmas tree, a Fisher-Price plastic basketball hoop, two pairs of ice skates, a Big Wheel, a cooler with a broken lid, two car tyres and four cardboard boxes of engine parts labelled *Randy's stuff*.

She was dragging out a lawnmower with two missing wheels when a black Audi A5 parked across the street. The driver's-side door opened and Gloria climbed out dressed in black jeans and a black leather coat, with a grey ski cap on her head. She walked past the junk men to where Lynette was standing. 'Why the fuck would you do it?' she screamed.

'What are you talking about?' said Lynette. She left the lawnmower by the truck and walked back to the garage. Gloria followed her.

'I know you stole my safe.'

Lynette stopped in the middle of the yard. 'Your safe? I didn't steal anything. What's wrong? Did you get robbed?'

'I've known you too long and you're a shitty liar.'

Lynette could smell wine on her breath. 'You really are a drunk, aren't you?'

'Fuck you,' Gloria yelled. 'I just want my safe.'

'I didn't even know you had a safe. Why would you have a safe?' Lynette turned and walked into the garage, bending down to grab a deflated soccer ball underneath the workbench. When she stood up, Gloria grabbed her by her coat collar.

'There's only one other person besides Terry who has a key and the code to my place. I was with Terry last night and my other friend promises it wasn't him. And you have the code and last night you were staying there. What am I supposed to think?'

'But I didn't stay there. I changed my mind and left the key on the counter. So get your hands off me.'

'Just give it back and I won't call the cops,' Gloria said, and let go of her coat.

'Call the cops? Call the cops for what? I left twenty minutes after you did. I didn't feel like being alone so I left.'

'You're such a fucking liar.'

'You better quit calling me a liar. And I don't have your safe.' Lynette put the soccer ball in a box that had a stack of rusted car chains in it, and picked it up. 'Why would I have your safe when I didn't even know you had one? Anyway, was it a big one?'

'Big enough.'

'Could you carry it?'

'No,' said Gloria.

'Then how could I carry it and where would I carry it to? You're crazy thinking it's me. And you can say you're not drunk but you smell like you're drunk and you're acting like you're drunk. So just leave me alone. I got a lot of things to do.' She left the box with the men, walked back to the garage and dragged out a Weber grill with no legs and no lid.

'I know you stole it,' Gloria said, still following her. 'It's why you're already losing your temper and you won't even look at me.'

Lynette stopped and turned around and glared at her. 'I'm not losing my temper and I'm looking straight at you. I'm sorry about your safe, I am, but I didn't steal it. I really didn't. What was in it, anyway?'

'You know what was in it.'

'Goddamn it!' yelled Lynette. 'I don't know.'

'Then I'm sure as fuck not telling you.'

'You owe me eight thousand dollars. Did you have that in your safe?'

'Fuck you. There was twice that in the safe and you know it.'

Lynette left the barbecue with the men and walked back toward the garage, then stopped. 'You're saying you had twice as much money as what you owed me and still you didn't give me anything? When I was begging? When I was begging for you to just pay me back what you owe me. Now you come here and have the nerve to say I stole it. And to think I gave you that eight thousand dollars as a friend. I gave it to you 'cause you're a fucking drunk and got a DUI.'

The junk men were now staring at them.

Gloria backed away from her. Her voice was shaking. 'I've done so much for you. Terry always said you were just leeching off me and he was right. And I've been so tired of hanging out with you. You live like a loser, still bartending at The Dutchman and you'll be there until you drop dead, just like your pal Shirley. Well, I fucking hate Shirley and you're just like her. I know you took the safe so give it back or I really will call the cops. There's a lot of personal things in it and I need those.'

In the garage Lynette took out a bike with missing tyres. It was blue with fluorescent-orange stripes. She'd bought it in high school at a garage sale, but the tyres had been stolen outside the Laurelhurst movie theatre when she was fifteen. Gloria followed her back and forth and Lynette kept making trips, and then finally she dropped a cardboard box of Christmas lights on the lawn.

'You told me you had no money. Last night I was hurting and I begged you for what you owe me and you didn't give me anything. You said you were broke. Fair enough if you were, but now it sounds like you weren't. I mean, why would you do that? I just don't understand why you'd do that to me. I've tried so hard to be a good friend. Do you remember when you called me, scared shitless, in jail? You were crying so hard you could barely talk. You begged me to pick you up and I did. I was the only real friend you had. You even told me that. And you were scared Terry would find out that you got a DUI and wouldn't like you any more and you were too broke to hire a lawyer and pay your fine. So who gave you eight thousand dollars without batting an eye?' She waited a moment but Gloria said nothing. 'Well, I did. And what about that time when you got so drunk you fell in your kitchen and cut your leg and had to go to the emergency room? You couldn't call Terry then either and you didn't want your other boyfriend to know. Or the time you got stranded in Salem with that weirdo businessman. You said you weren't seeing any other men, but you always are. You didn't want Terry to find out. So I came and got you. I beat on the hotel room door and then came in and got you out of the bathroom where you were hiding . . . Jesus, I'm stupid. You can call the cops if you want. Bring over a SWAT team and have them tear the house down looking for it. But your safe isn't here.'

'You're just trying to depress me,' said Gloria. Lynette noticed the make-up on her face had been put on too thick and her lipstick was a bit off, as was her eyeliner. 'That's all you're doing. Always bringing up my past, bringing up things that aren't really me, that aren't who I really am. You always try to pull me down this way. Terry thinks you're jealous of me 'cause you're always broke and you drive a shitty car and live in a dump. He thinks you want to be me and that's why you're such a leech. I always told him he wasn't right, but I think he is right.'

'Look,' said Lynette, 'you didn't go to Catlin Gabel private school and you sure as fuck didn't go to Berkeley. So if I remind you that you grew up in Clatskanie in a trailer and had to get your GED to graduate high school and that you even flunked out of flight attendant school, it's because that's who you are. And you can't get rid of that, no matter how much shit you buy. You're a prostitute, I'm a prostitute. But I've tried to be your friend, your real friend, and you fucked me. You basically stole from me. So please just leave me alone and if you keep bothering me I'll call Terry and I'll tell him to look for your Catlin Gabel yearbook and I'll tell him you didn't go to Berkeley.'

Gloria began pacing back and forth. 'Why would you do that? Why would you ruin me? I mean, just give me back the safe and you can have the eight grand. I'm sorry I didn't give it to you last night. I should have but I was in a hurry. But I swear I'll give you the money I owe you. And I'll even give you a grand extra as interest. Just give me back the safe.'

Lynette grabbed her by the coat. 'Look, I don't have your safe. I don't know how many times I got to tell you.'

'I know you have it, I know it, so just give it back to me. There's pictures I want, and jewellery.'

Lynette turned and saw Kenny walking toward her. The front door was open and he looked past her as one of the junk men picked up his Big Wheel and threw it over the metal railing and into the back of the truck. He screamed in horror when he saw it and jogged toward the truck and the two men.

Lynette ran to him to keep him off the street. She put her arm around him. 'It's okay,' she said gently. 'Don't get upset. You know you can't fit on the Big Wheel any more. We've tried and tried but you can't. We'll find you a better thing. I promise. But let these guys get back to work, 'cause they're workmen and you like workmen.'

Kenny was dressed in his red Trail Blazers sweat suit. He couldn't stop crying and then a dark spot appeared from his crotch and ran down his leg.

Gloria walked to the sidewalk where they were standing. 'I want my goddamn safe.'

'Jesus, I don't have it,' cried Lynette. 'Check the house if you want. Call the cops if you want, but just leave us alone.'

Gloria shook in anger. 'You and your fucked-up brother, and your nutjob mom. Well, I'm calling the cops and they'll fucking throw you all in prison and I hope you rot there for the rest of your lives.' She flipped Lynette off then walked across the street, got into her car and left.

20

The junk men left and Lynette gave Kenny a shower, put clean clothes on him, made him another peanut-butter-and-jam sandwich and sat him on the couch with a *Brave* DVD. In the kitchen she used her mother's landline and called JJ's home phone. Once again it was answered by the pregnant girl. The TV was on in the background and Lynette waited for a long time before JJ came on the line.

'What the fuck did you do?' he asked in a groggy voice.

'What did I do?' she said as quiet as she could. 'I know you don't like me but you could have gotten me killed. That guy is really crazy. And I paid you back for the abortion. I even gave you extra money for doing it. I know it took me a while, but I was in a bad way. I had to get a job again and then save money. But I paid you back and you know I did because I called to make sure you got it and you said you did. And when we lived together I worked at your store for free and I cooked and cleaned your house. I paid my way and you know I did because you always said it. You always said that I did more than I had to. And after all you put me through, why would you set me up like that? I mean, I just don't understand.'

'I didn't think it would get so out of hand,' he said. 'I didn't think you'd Mace him.'

'He pulled a gun on me – what was I supposed to do? He said you owed him money and this was the way you'd get out of debt. He said you guys had planned it out.'

'I do owe him money,' JJ said, and coughed. 'And now, thanks to you, I have to pay him back. I've owed him a couple grand for three years. I thought he forgot about it. But then when I called him to set things up for you, he reminded me what I owed him and I thought maybe it could work out, that he'd just give you a grand or two and you'd be alright with that and he'd be alright and I wouldn't have to deal with getting him his money. Now he says I got to give him the two grand by the end of next week or he's gonna come over and take it. Thing is, I don't have two grand and my mom is on a European cruise and I can't get a hold of her.'

'That's not my fault.'

'Maybe, but he's asking me where you live.'

Lynette put her elbows on the kitchen table and sighed. 'So what should I do?'

'I don't know,' he said. 'I don't know how pissed off he really is.'

She paused for a time and then said, 'If I give you the money, the two grand, will you tell him to leave me alone? I'd give it to him myself but I don't want to be near him again. The thing is, I know he'll find out where I live and I don't want him to bother my mom. Will you call him and ask him if that'll be okay? And you have to tell him the truth. You have to tell him I didn't owe you anything. That it wasn't my fault. I mean, he's the one who pulled a gun on me. He forced it to go that way, not me. Will you promise to tell him that if I give you the money and his gun back?'

JJ again coughed and she could hear him light a cigarette. 'I'll tell him but the thing is, it wasn't just two grand. It was closer to three. I think I could get him off your back for three.'

'Three?'

'Yeah.'

'I'll give you three,' Lynette said, her voice growing sadder. 'I'll give it to you.'

★

In a shoebox of papers she found the registration to her car and while Kenny watched his movie she moved the Sentra to the carport and took the money from the trunk and her personal things out of it. A wrecking yard on Columbia Boulevard said they would take it if she brought it to them by five, so when she was finished, she and Kenny left. First she drove to JJ's and gave him three thousand dollars and Rodney's gun. After that she drove to the post office on Killingsworth. On an overnight box she wrote Gloria's address with her left hand. The writing was crude but legible. She put no note inside, only the nine thousand dollars, the personal papers, the photos, the jewellery and the silver dollars.

At B&R Auto Wrecking she gave them the title and the keys and they gave her two hundred dollars cash for the car. It was 4.50 p.m. and raining and already dark. From there she and Kenny took a Radio Cab to Stark Street Pizza. Lynette ordered a medium pepperoni and two Cokes and they sat by the video games and ate.

182

It was night and still raining when the cab stopped in front of their home. The white Avalon was in the carport, the porch light was on, and Lynette and Kenny went inside to find their mother on the couch watching TV and smoking a cigarette. Kenny went to her and she muted the sound and said, 'My God, how did you clean so fast?'

Lynette put her purse on the table near the front door and sat in the wooden chair. 'I got one of those trucks that say they move junk. Those guys take anything and they loaded it all. I also went to the Goodwill a bunch. I got rid of almost all my clothes.'

'I want to get rid of all mine too. I hate everything I wear,' her mother said, half-looking at the TV. 'How's your back?'

'It's been hurting all day because of moving but I think I'm okay,' said Lynette. 'My ribs hurt worse than the cuts.'

'They say rib injuries are the most painful. You want me to redo your bandages?'

'Would you mind?'

Her mother put out her cigarette. 'I bought more bandages and more hydrogen peroxide,' she said, and took the electric blanket off herself, put it on Kenny and stood up.

Lynette turned up the thermostat and her mother grabbed the plastic bag from Walgreens and followed her to the bathroom, then helped her off with her shirt. Lynette sat on the toilet.

'Jesus, you got beat up. The bruises are really showing now.'

'I know,' whispered Lynette.

Her mother sat on the edge of the bathtub and took the

gauze, white tape and bottle of hydrogen peroxide from the bag.

'What did you do today?' asked Lynette.

'I went over to Mona's house,' her mother said. 'Do you remember her?'

'You used to work with her, right?'

'Yeah, for about five years. I'd guess that was maybe fifteen years ago. You probably remember her husband.'

'I'm not sure.'

Her mother took off the large gauze bandages. One wound was completely covered with dry blood and looked better, but the other was still open and looked infected already. 'We went out on his boat once,' she said. 'He's the guy who wore the too-tight swim trunks and the golf shirts and had the huge belly. One of those guys who looked pregnant.'

'Did he smoke a pipe?'

'Yeah, that's him. Mona said when he died he weighed close to four hundred pounds. Can you imagine carrying that around? Jesus, he must have been tired all the time. They had to hire men to get him out of the house. Mona said they have services like that now. Weightlifting strongmen to pick up fat people who die at home. She said they have the same thing at hospitals too. Weightlifters to move fatsos around. I don't know why everyone's getting so fat, but they sure are. A lady who comes by the store, Rayleen, once told me, she said, "Sometimes all you can do in life is have another bowl of ice cream. Sometimes that's the only move you can make to keep yourself from going completely nuts." Maybe she's right.

Boy, they'll sure get a workout with me, the way things are going. You'll see, when it hits it hits and there ain't much you can do about it. Anyway, Mona's husband had a heart attack watching TV. Mona was in the room with him at the time. Can you imagine? What an awful thing to see. I don't know if you remember, but Mona said she hurt her back at work. I mean, my God, how do you hurt your back working at a jewellery store? But after a lot of paperwork bullshit she got the claim. Every month she gets a check. She's pretty savvy that way. Seven hundred and thirty-five bucks a month, plus she's getting her husband's social security check. It's only eight hundred 'cause she's claiming it early and he never made any real money in his life. Still, together it's a decent amount. But the thing is, over the years they mortgaged their house and then remortgaged it again. They added a deck, put in a hot tub and he bought that boat we went on. So now she owes on the house even though they've had it for more than thirty years. So I was talking with her a while back. She said she was struggling to pay the mortgage on her own and scared she would have to get a job again, so after a lot of back and forth, I told her I'd help her out.' Her mother paused and then said uncertainly, 'I'm gonna move in with her.'

'Really?' said Lynette.

Her mother finished taking off the smaller bandages. 'Hey, only a couple of the cuts still look bad. The big one near your right shoulder looks like something might still be in it.' She pressed near it. 'Do you feel that area?'

'Yeah.'

'Is it more painful than the other?'

'Yeah.'

'I think we might have to try and clean it out again. There might be something still in there. I'll get my glasses.'

Her mother got up and left the room and came back with reading glasses and her bedside lamp. She plugged it in and pointed it at Lynette's back and then went to the medicine cabinet and found the tweezers. She washed them in the sink. 'This is probably gonna hurt.'

'That's okay,' said Lynette. 'Where is Mona's house?'

'You know where Gartner's Meats is on Killingsworth?'

'I think so.'

'It's across the road by Glenwood trailer park. It's not the best part of town. It's not even a real neighbourhood but she says she's never had a break-in. I'm surprised about that, but that's what she says.' Her mother poured hydrogen peroxide on the cut and wiped it off with toilet paper. 'I'm gonna pull it apart some. So get ready.'

'I'm ready.'

'Okay, I'm going to do it now.' Her mother pulled the cut apart and Lynette cried out. 'I'm sorry, baby. Just a little bit more. I think I missed a piece. I think I see something.' She took the tweezers and pulled out a thin sliver of glass and put it in the sink. She looked around the cut once more. 'I think I got it. I think that's it,' she said, and again rinsed it with peroxide.

'What's Mona like? I can't really remember her.'

'She's alright, she's got a good sense of humour, but she's kind of a moper. A real "Why me?" sorta person. She's the type who would complain if she won the lottery because she'd have to go through traffic to collect her ten million dollars.'

Lynette laughed. 'And you want to live with her?'

'It's cheap and I do like her and I don't have to come up with a deposit. Everything's in her name and she doesn't want anything upfront. She and I have been talking about living together for a while.'

'For a while?'

'Just talking. You know how I am.' Her mother took a dish towel from a shelf near the door and soaked it with peroxide and wiped the other cuts on Lynette's back. 'How you holding up?'

'It hurts but I'm alright. What's her house like?'

'It's not much. I think her husband built the place and he wasn't much of a carpenter. None of the doors shut right and half the windows don't open. There's carpet but it's maroon shag. It's that real bushy kind, maybe two inches high, and I don't think you can really get that kind of carpet clean. And if you ask me, it's ugly, but she loves the colour red. I've never seen a person like one colour that much. She even picked out my lipstick. Look?'

Lynette turned around to see dark-red lipstick on her mother's lips. 'I like that colour. It looks good on you.'

'I like it too,' her mother said, picking up the bedside lamp and once again looking over the cuts. 'I think we're almost done. The one on your shoulder is the only one to worry about, but I think I got all the glass out of it this time. Now all I have to do is put Neosporin on and then the Band-Aids and then the two bandages. So just keep holding tough.'

'Thanks,' said Lynette. 'How big is her place?'

'Smaller than ours. No basement either. Her washer and dryer are in the garage but they're new so that'll be nice. The house has a good hot-water heater and a heat pump. I'm not sure how those things work but it's always warm and Mona likes it warm and she says it doesn't cost much to keep it that way.'

'And you'll have your own room?'

Her mother put Band-Aids on the smaller cuts and started in on the gauze pads and white tape on the larger ones. 'Yeah. It's pretty big and has a sliding glass door that opens onto a deck. The deck just looks out over her yard, though, which is mostly blackberry bushes. Behind her fence is some sort of construction business. I think they do scaffolding. A bunch of trucks and things like that. I probably won't go out there except to smoke. She doesn't like smoking in the house but I guess nobody does any more. She has a hot tub on the deck too, but it's broken. I guess a pipe broke and Mona won't fix it.' Her mother finished taping the last bandage. 'Alright, we're done,' she said.

Lynette sighed.

'It still hurts, huh?'

'Yeah.'

Her mother put the cap on the peroxide and threw the dish towel and the used Band-Aids and bandages in the trash basket. She put the box of bandages, Band-Aids, peroxide and Neosporin in the Walgreens bag. 'Do you need help with your shirt?'

'Yeah.'

Her mother helped her put it on and said, 'Take the bag with you. You'll need to change them again. Where are you staying tonight?'

'I don't know.'

'You can stay on the couch or in my bed. Kenny won't mind a sleeping bag on the floor.'

Lynette got up and followed her mother out to the living room and sat in the same wooden chair by the door.

Her mother sat next to Kenny on the couch and put the electric blanket over them both. 'The good news is Mona has a neighbour who is a hair stylist. She said she can get me a makeover pretty cheap and Jesus knows I could use one. Plus she said she'll shop for me online. I've never been good at buying online but she says you can get stuff and try it on and if you don't like it you can send it back for free. I didn't know that. And she has another friend who will do my nails for ten bucks a pop.'

'I didn't know you talked to Mona so much. I haven't heard her name in a long time. When did you guys start being friends again?'

'We never really quit talking, we've just been talking more lately.'

'"Lately" meaning how long?'

Her mother shrugged, took her cigarettes from the coffee table and lit one.

'Can I ask you a question?'

'Maybe,' said her mother.

'Did you ever want to buy the house?' she said, almost in a whisper. 'I mean, were you ever really serious about us buying it?'

Her mother blew out a trail of smoke and sighed. 'I don't know . . . Maybe. Maybe I was at one point. But it was all too much for me and I don't want to get into that again. I'm exhausted and I don't have it in me to see you get upset again.'

'Why can't I be upset? Because I'm just beginning to realize you were never serious about buying the house. You watched me work so hard I could barely see straight and, even so, you didn't say anything. Not a word that you didn't want the house.'

'If I would have, you would have just yelled at me.'

'That's not fair.'

'Well, the money you made is still yours, isn't it? And if you honestly do have almost a hundred thousand then that's something. That's a lot more than I have and I'll tell you this, I sure didn't have that when I was your age. I just had two babies and a deadbeat husband. But you, you get all that money for yourself and I'm not even asking for any of it. And I could ask for some, I could, I could ask for a lot, but I won't because I want you to have a chance. You deserve a chance, but then I deserve a chance too . . . I have to tell you something else. Something I was gonna tell you tomorrow when I wasn't so tired but I guess I'll tell you now and get it over with. And I want you to listen to me before you say anything. Listen to me all the way through before you interrupt and get upset. Can you do that?'

Lynette nodded.

'You promise?'

'I promise, I won't interrupt.'

Her mother knocked the ash from her cigarette onto a plate sitting on the coffee table. 'For all the bad things I've said about Mona, she's also smart and she can really work the system. She studies it, and today she and I came up with a plan. The way she figures it, I can become a PCA caregiver. I can get hired as Kenny's full-time caregiver. I'll have to get interviewed first and they'll have to check out Mona's place, but what it means is that I can get fourteen sixty-five an hour, twenty hours a week, from the State of Oregon to look after Kenny. That's about a thousand bucks a month. But, see, I won't do it. Mona will, at least most of it. That way she can keep her disability check. And, on top of that, I'll get Kenny's monthly disability check and his food stamps. The arrangement is that she gets the PCA money, I don't pay rent, only half of the utilities, and I give her Kenny's food stamps. She'll give those to her fucked-up daughter and she'll look after Kenny while I'm at work. This way I can finally save some money. It's kind of confusing and I'm not sure I totally understand but I think it can work and it'll be a good opportunity for me. Plus she said she'd give me half of her food stamps if I do the shopping. She's one of those people who hates leaving the house. She hasn't eaten in a restaurant in over a year, hasn't gone to the mall or anything. What are they called?'

'Agoraphobics.'

'Well, she's that. The only problem is that her house only has two bedrooms so Kenny and I have to share a room. But I sleep on the couch most nights anyway so basically he'll get his own room. After about eight Mona goes into her room and she's got her own bathroom in there and doesn't come out until eleven or twelve the next morning.'

'But you're forgetting something,' said Lynette. 'I'm taking Kenny. That was the deal.'

'Well, I've changed my mind.'

'You can't just change your mind.'

'I can because he's my son, not yours.'

'I won't let you.'

Her mother let out a short laugh. 'What are you gonna do?'

'I'll fight for custody.'

'And tell them what? That you've got anger issues, that you've tried to kill yourself, that you've been hospitalized for it, and that most likely, from what I gather, you've been making money in a way I don't even want to think about.'

'You'd tell them all that?'

Her mother shrugged.

Tears welled in Lynette's eyes and she didn't say anything. She wanted to argue, she wanted to stand up to her mother, but it all just flooded over her like concrete. The guilt and shame of what she'd done and what had been done to her. It took the wind from her, and so she just sat there.

Her mother took a drag from her cigarette and moved closer to Kenny. 'And you don't even have a place to live. How can you get custody with no home?'

'That's not fair. You're being really cruel now.'

'I'm sorry . . . You say I haven't given a shit about Kenny in years. Maybe that's true but what have you done? All you do is work. You said so yourself.'

'But I'm not gonna be like that any more,' said Lynette. 'I don't have to be. I just did that for us, for the house.'

'You did it so you could have a house. I'll be long dead before any mortgage would have ever been paid up.'

'I wanted the house for all of us and I did everything for us, not for me. And you know that's true.'

'Maybe. Maybe you did,' her mother said. 'And maybe I've fucked up everything in our lives, maybe the whole problem from the get-go is me. Is that what you want to hear? Does it make you feel better to hear that? Well, it's probably true anyway, and that's a hard thing to realize. I mean, I picked your dad even when I knew he was gonna ruin me. I was telling Mona that I knew by our third date he was no good, that he was a low-down fucker. Did you know he borrowed fifty bucks from me on our third date? Fifty bucks and he never paid me back. Can you imagine? Third date and already he's stealing from me. But Jesus, he was so handsome and charming and good in bed and all that shit you think is interesting when you're young. But even so, what the hell was I thinking? My dad couldn't believe it. He kept saying, "Doreen, what are you doing with him? Are you sure he's the right one? Are you certain? Don't you think a girl should shop around before she gets too involved with one boy?" My dad knew your dad was a no-good idiot. Did I ever tell you about the time we all went to Old Town Pizza?'

'I'm not sure,' said Lynette.

'I told Mona this not too long ago. It was my mom and dad and your father. We'd been together maybe six months by then. Your father showed up drunk and kept drinking. He ordered a pitcher of beer and then he spilled it on the pizza. In my whole life I've never seen that before. Somebody spilling a full pitcher of beer on a pizza. And do you know what he did when he spilled it? He started screaming at the kid trying to clean up the mess. He blamed the spilling of the pitcher on a kid who was bussing another table when it happened. Your father demanded a free pizza and another pitcher of beer. My God, it was awful, so embarrassing. Dad took me aside a week later. He was worried. He said a guy who'd do that would probably be the kind of guy who could make your life pretty tough. He said it was a small thing by itself but it meant something bigger. I yelled at Dad for saying bad things about him, but of course he was right.'

'I miss Grandpa every day,' Lynette said, and went to the coffee table, took a cigarette from her mother's pack, lit it and sat back down in the chair.

'Me too,' her mother said. 'He was a good man. They always say the only way you can find a good man is to be raised by a good man. That sure hasn't worked for me. I didn't land close to the tree that way. I'm starting to think some people are just born to sink. Born to fail. And I'm beginning to realize I'm one of those people, and you have no idea what that's like. How truly awful it is to know that about yourself. But that doesn't mean I want things as hard as they've been. And it doesn't mean I want it to stay that way. It doesn't mean I like it either. But I got to live too, don't I?'

21

Lynette waited under the carport until the cab came. The driver took her down Interstate to Lombard and then to Pier Park in St Johns and dropped her off. The duplex was a ranch-style single-level and had recently been painted. The left side had its porch light on and Lynette walked up the concrete walkway and knocked on the door. Two dogs barked from inside, the door opened, and the old woman, Shirley, stood in front of Lynette holding a bottle of Coors Light.

Inside, a small lamp sat on a table in the corner of the living room and gave off the only light besides the TV. Shirley was dressed in green sweats that read *University of Oregon*. On her feet were green-and-yellow slippers. A Burgerville bag sat on the coffee table. Her dogs, Bernese mountain dogs, continued to bark until Shirley called for them to stop.

'You want a drink?' she asked.

'Sure,' said Lynette, taking off her coat and hanging it on a hook by the door.

'I have your bottle of Jägermeister in the freezer. You still drinking that?'

'Yeah.'

'Then just help yourself.'

Lynette went to the kitchen and poured a drink. Shirley went back to the couch and her two dogs jumped up on either side of her. Lynette sat in a recliner next to them. Behind Shirley, on the back wall, was an enlarged colour photo of her father's logging truck. It was from the 1960s and the photo showed the entire length of a dented and faded blue Kenworth pulling a trailer of logs. On the door it read *V&P Logging, Vernonia, OR.*

Shirley turned off the TV and put her arm around one of her dogs. 'So what's going on? First crying all day and now calling out of the blue wanting to buy my dad's car.'

'Are you still okay with selling it to me?'

'Yeah, of course.' She nodded. 'But, like I said, it smells of cigars. I took it to one of those places but even they couldn't get the smell out. It only has thirty thousand miles on it but still no one wants it. I've had it on Craigslist for a month. It's a 2003 Buick LeSabre. A real old man's car. You want to look at it now?'

'Not yet.'

Shirley took a drink of beer. 'Then are you going to tell me what's going on?'

Lynette petted the dog closest to her. 'My mom backed out of buying the house.'

'She backed out?' said Shirley. 'Really backed out or is she just being nervous?'

Lynette shook her head, looked down and whispered, 'We're not going to get the house and tonight I learned that I don't think she was ever serious about buying it. Not really . . . But the thing is, she never told me she wasn't serious. I don't know why she wouldn't tell me, but she didn't. For over three years I worked two jobs and I had the other thing also.'

'Jesus, I'm sorry.'

'I worked so hard, Shirley, I could barely breathe,' Lynette whispered.

'I know you did,' she said gently.

Lynette looked her. 'She doesn't want to live with me, Shirley. That's why she doesn't want the house. That's the reason. She doesn't want to be near me any more.'

Shirley took another sip of her beer and set it down on the coffee table. 'In the end, maybe that's a good thing.'

'How can that be a good thing?'

'Because living with her isn't good for you.'

'Maybe,' said Lynette. 'Maybe . . . You know, she wanted me to take Kenny, and I wanted to, but now she's keeping him. She's even taking him away from me. She says she'll tell everyone I'm unfit if I try to get custody.' Lynette wiped tears from her face with her hands. 'I'm sorry. I don't mean to cry in front of you.'

'It's okay. When I saw your face yesterday I knew something was up. I'd have thought you were pregnant or your boyfriend left you or someone in your family died. But I've never seen you with a boyfriend and you wouldn't be lucky enough to have someone in your family die.' She smiled. 'What are you going to do?'

'I'm not sure,' said Lynette, and leaned over and rested her elbows on her legs. 'My head feels like it's imploding, you know?'

'Yeah, I know,' said Shirley.

Lynette again wiped her eyes.

'Well, at least now you can be done with that one thing, right? No more Gloria?'

'No, no more of that,' said Lynette. 'I just didn't know how else to make that kind of money. And it was easy at first because Gloria set it all up. But it got harder the longer I did it. No, I won't do that again.'

'I'm not judging you,' said Shirley. 'I just don't think it's a smart thing for someone like you. For Gloria I don't think it matters because she's always been a taker. But underneath it all you're a good person and you're too sensitive and you worry too much about what people think to do that for a living and not have it ruin you. It'll ruin Gloria, but that's because Gloria's lazy. That's different. Do you promise me you'll never do it again?'

'I promise.'

'Good. That makes me feel good.'

'And I think I'm gonna have to leave town.'

'Leave town? Where?'

'I don't know. But if I stay here I'll probably just have to get a room somewhere. An apartment, even a studio, is around thirteen hundred bucks a month and I'll work all day just to scrape by living in it. I'll never be able to buy a house. I know I always told you that I dreamed about owning a bakery, like the Tulip Pastry Shop when it was open. I wasn't joking about that. Before our landlord gave us notice, that was my plan. I was saving money for that. Not a lot of money but I had some. I was an idiot to think I could ever do that. Because there's no way I'll ever get the amount of money together to open one here. Never. I mean, my landlord says he thinks they'll get three hundred thousand for the house I grew up in. And I mean, you've been there.'

'The house two doors down from here went for four hundred and thirty. It's crazy. I don't know what to tell you about that. I just got lucky. I was just here when it wasn't expensive, and when my husband got sick he sold our house and bought the duplex for me so I'd have income. But me, I never saved anything. I always spent it as quick as I got it. But my husband was smarter, he set me up alright.' She paused for a moment and then said, 'You know, I read in the paper a while ago that the places to move are in the Midwest. That it's cheap in the old cities. Like St Louis or Kansas City or Detroit or Cleveland. Everyone left them for a while but now people are going back. Maybe you could start a bakery out there. In some city like that. How much money you got?'

'Almost a hundred thousand.'

'Well, that's something, isn't it? Just work on fixing your credit, talk to somebody on how to do it, and save that money and then buy something.'

'Is it stupid to still want to buy something?' Lynette said, and took a drink.

'I don't know. I'm not that smart about things like that. But we were all brought up to think it's the only way not to be broke. The American dream, you know? Maybe that's all changing, but for you, I think you should buy something because it'll give you something to work for. Something of your own. And you need something of your own. But maybe you should just stay here for a while and think it over. You could live with me for a few months.'

'Thank you,' said Lynette, and again tears fell down her face. 'But I can't stay here. This is just down the street from where I lived with Jack. I don't even like walking through St Johns any more. I don't even like going over the bridge and it's my favourite bridge in the world. I'm realizing that the whole city is starting to haunt me. And all the new places, all the new big buildings, just remind me that I'm nothing, that I'm nobody.'

Shirley finished her beer, got up, went to the fridge, opened another and came back with the bottle of Jäger-meister and set it on the table in front of Lynette. 'Maybe you should use the money and go to college. Everybody goes to college now.'

Lynette laughed and looked at a picture on a shelf near the TV. It was of Shirley and her husband on a beach. They were both wearing swimsuits and smiling with their arms around each other. In the picture Shirley was even younger than Lynette. 'It took me a year to get my GED. That was hard enough. I've taken three classes at PCC and for all of them I studied harder than I ever studied for anything and still I only barely passed. No . . . I just don't think I'm smart enough.'

'Then maybe a bakery is the right move. You do make the best cakes I've ever had, and cookies and those little pie things.'

'Crostatas?'

'Yeah, I'd almost kill somebody for one of those right now.'

'Thank you, Shirley.'

'And if you really do have to leave town, don't worry about The Dutchman. I'll cover the shifts I can and you know Wendy's wanted your slot for a couple years.'

'I know. I already called her,' said Lynette, and poured herself a short drink from the bottle.

Shirley put her arm around the dog to the right of her. 'I'm gonna be straight with you, okay? Take it however you want but I'm gonna be straight because I like you. You were in trouble with Gloria. I knew it but I didn't say anything because I knew why you were doing it. Well, now you're free of that. That's a lucky thing. And I love your brother, he's a sweetheart, and I know you're scared to be without him, but ain't it time for you to be your own person? Haven't you done enough for him? Your mom is right on one thing – he's her son. She has legal rights over him. Not you. And I will say this too: I'm relieved that your mom backed out of the house. I'm really happy for you because you would have been handcuffed to her for the rest of her life. And you don't deserve that. I've known your mom a lot of years. As you know, I knew her when she was married to your dad. And in the three years you've worked at The Dutchman, she's never once come in while you're working, but she comes in while I'm working because she knows I'll give her free drinks. After a while I started writing down the number of free drinks. I've given her over a hundred free lemon drops and she's never once tipped or asked to pay. And all she's ever done when she's there is bitch. Just complain about things, about her job, you, your brother, your dad. That says enough to me about who she is.'

Lynette nodded. She leaned back in her recliner and closed her eyes.

'You know, I never had kids.'

Lynette opened her eyes. 'Did you want them?'

'Sure. I went crazy about it for a while. My husband wanted them too. But I couldn't have them. But if I had a daughter, I always thought I'd want her to be like you.'

'Like me?' Lynette said, and then whispered, 'But I'm no good at all. I've done a lot of bad things, Shirley.'

'Not really, you haven't. Not to me. See, the thing is, you never give up and you got a good heart, a damaged heart, but a good heart, and you want to do good. Most people don't care about doing good. Most people just push you out of the way and grab what they want.'

Lynette began crying again. 'That's the nicest thing anyone's ever said to me.'

Shirley stood up. 'I'm gonna start crying too, and I hate crying. The older I get the more I hate it. So let's go see your new car. But here's the thing I've decided. I ain't gonna sell it. I'm giving it to you. And I don't want any arguments about it. I don't want any discussion and I don't want you leaving money in my mailbox either. Just let me do it. It's my way of wishing you luck in life. My dad was a nice guy, even though he smoked cigars. He'd want you to have it. He had a thing about brunettes.'

22

The car was a silver four-door sedan and it started on the first try. Lynette left Shirley's with the title in the glovebox and drove down the street and passed the house she'd lived in with Jack. Inside, the lights were on and she could see a woman sitting at a table near the kitchen. She glanced at it for a moment, hoping she'd never in her life have to see the house or think about it again. She made it to Lombard Street and headed south, past the now-closed Tulip Pastry Shop, and left St Johns.

It was 10 p.m. when she parked in front of her house. Inside, her mother was watching TV and smoking a cigarette. A pint of gin and a bottle of tonic were on the coffee table. Lynette set her purse on the table by the door and sat down in the same chair she always sat in.

'Where'd you go?' asked her mother.

'I bought Shirley's old car.'

'Her car? What kind?'

'It's a 2003 Buick. It's a boat but it drives nice.'

'Got rid of the Nissan?'

'I took it to the wrecking yard today. You getting drunk?'

Her mother shrugged. 'Just having a drink.'

'Where's Kenny?'

'In my room.'

'I'm gonna start loading things out.'

'You don't have to leave tonight.'

'I'll lose my nerve if I don't leave tonight.'

'Where you gonna go?'

'I don't know.'

Her mother turned the sound down on the TV and took a drink from her Trail Blazers cup. 'I've been thinking a lot today,' she said. 'You might say I don't love you, but I do love you. I love you because you're my daughter. I'd run in front of a bus to save you. Right this second I would and every second you've been breathing. I've always felt that way. You wouldn't understand that, the way a mother feels about her kids. I'd give my life to save yours until the day I keel over. That's the truth. But really, that doesn't mean I have to like you or that we have to get along or that you even have to like me. 'Cause I'd guess you haven't liked me in a lot of years.'

'It's not that I haven't liked you. I never think that way. I don't know why you always say things like that.'

'Well . . . We're like oil and water. That's what they say, right?'

'That's what they say.'

Her mother poured gin into her Trail Blazers cup and filled it to the top with tonic. She stirred it with her finger. 'Anyway, I've been thinking and before you start getting upset and start bringing up Kenny, let me tell you one more time the basic fact. You're not his mother. I know you think I don't care about him any more and that now I'm using him for his money, but the truth is he's ruled my life since the moment he was born. Ruled it. Now I'm worn out. So don't I deserve a little something for that? Some sorta payment? Even just a bit?' She took another drink and kept it in her hand. She kept her eyes on the TV. 'Maybe you should hate my guts and maybe I deserve to get my head caved in by you. Maybe that wouldn't be the worst thing that happened, but really, in the end, where would that leave us – you, me and Kenny? Nowhere, that's where. We have to get by regardless of what we feel. And I'm gonna be honest with you right now. So you have to listen to me. Will you do that?'

'I'm listening.'

'I have even less hours coming in. I've been averaging twenty-seven hours a week for the last three months. I've known for a while I have to get a second job and I've put in applications. But Christ, I'm old, and no one wants to hire a worn-out middle-aged fatso. Most of the time now when my alarm goes off I just want to give up. That's the truth. I've almost lost hope. I know that sounds horrible, maybe I'm being too dramatic, but it's the way I feel. I'm not trying to whine or complain. I'm just telling you how it is because who knows how much we'll really talk after tonight. The thing is, Lynette, I'm getting mean. Not angry like you, but just mean and bitter. And on the TV . . . All these rich sons of bitches, they just talk bullshit and take whatever they want. They take and take and then, when they get themselves in a pickle, we bail them out. So why would they care about anything but themselves? The politicians don't give a shit times a thousand. All they want to do is stay elected. And when they get re-elected, they still don't get anything done. They don't seem to want to help anybody and they have no backbone. They just argue and blame and take money and get great healthcare while they do it. Those cocksuckers get free healthcare and we don't. They don't even care about our health. That says a lot, doesn't it? So why vote? I'm serious. Why? Because they don't do anything. They don't help. And if they don't help then what's the point of any of them?'

She looked at Lynette and took another drink.

'Do you think Fred Meyer gives a shit about me? They give me enough hours so it's a pain in the ass for me to get another job but not enough hours that I can get by. So why should I do them any favours? Why should I be loyal to them? They'll drop me whenever they want and not think about it for a half a second. So if I fudge a few hours here and there or something goes missing and ends up in my purse, why should it matter to me? Because I don't matter to them. So I'll screw them any chance I can.'

'Look, I know you've had it tough,' said Lynette, 'but right now you should just go to bed. We're both tired and you're drunk.'

Her mother shook her head. 'I'm not drunk. I know what I'm saying. So will you listen to me? Will you really listen?'

'I'm listening,' said Lynette.

'Last month Mona and I drove around downtown. Near where your bakery is. The Pearl District. When I was your age no one went to that part of town. It was all empty buildings and bums and guys shooting up. Now, as you know, it's all fancy buildings and skinny people who look like they're in magazines. I don't know where they all come from but they sure are coming. And then . . . Then all you do is cross another street and there's

206

homeless people camping everywhere. They're coming too. You can't drive around Portland without seeing a hundred tents. People living in tents! Are they all on drugs? Are there that many people who are crazy and on drugs? I used to always ask myself, Why would a man in his twenties want to live on the street when he could work? I mean, my God, what's happening? For a long time I didn't understand it. Why, why would they live that way? It seems so awful. So miserable. But, you know, now I think I'm starting to understand. The answer is: why not? Why should they bust their ass all day when they know no matter what they do they'll never get ahead. And why should they pay three hundred thousand for a falling-down shack when they don't have to? And when it starts raining and getting cold and they get sick, well, they'll be the first ones who march up to any hospital and get taken in. Me, I have to pay for my shitty health insurance and all the goddamn co-pays, and I have to pay out the nose for anything that's not covered, and there's a lot of things not covered. And then some home-less creep who lives in a tent just goes to the hospital and gets everything for free. Politicians get healthcare for free and bums do too. But of course not us. How does that make sense? How does that make you want to get out of bed in the morning and go to work and stand next to Cheryl? Christ . . . So there we are, me and Mona driving around downtown. We go from Naito Parkway to 11th Avenue and every place in between. The whole time we're just wondering who can afford to live in these fancy new high-rises and where do they get the money to eat in all these new restaurants? I mean, how do you pay three hundred dollars for a pair of shoes or five thousand dollars for a couch? I just don't understand, for the life of me, where so many people get their money. And what am I supposed to do? Go to college? Learn about computers? I'm old. So I guess I'm what you'd call a loser . . . Jesus, I'm a loser. But knowing it doesn't change anything.'

She stopped, lit a cigarette and took a long drag from it. Her eyes were wild and she was sweating even though the room was barely sixty degrees.

'Why don't you go to sleep now,' said Lynette.

'I don't want to go to sleep,' her mother said, and rested the cigarette in the ashtray. 'I'm just trying to tell you the way it is.' She took another drink and went on. 'You say you have almost a hundred thousand dollars. Well, I have my ideas on how you got the money, and I'm pretty sure my ideas are the truth. But I'm not judging. Why should I? It's back to what I've been thinking every moment I'm awake lately. What does it matter? What does it matter if you slept with some rich guy so he'd give you enough money to get what you need? What does it matter to any-one else but you? And why should it bother you? The rich son of a bitch probably thinks he's getting one over on you, but you're getting one over on him too. That's what's been bothering me lately. Why does it matter to feel bad about anything? Isn't that the American dream? Fuck over whoever is in your way and get what you want. I barely got through high school but if I remember anything about history, I remember that. The people who are remembered are the ones taking. People arrive somewhere and try to get their piece. They don't care who they hurt doing it, they really don't, and I'm starting to understand why. Because it's all bullshit. The land of the free and that whole crock of shit. It's just men taking what they want and justifying it any way they need to so they can get up in the morning and take more and buy another speedboat and their third vacation home and their fifth rental property and then push people out of their homes so they can make more money and go on safaris and kill giraffes and elephants all while everyone else is just trying to pay off their credit card bill or student loan or trying to get enough hours at one job so they don't have to get a second. Well, fine then. If they're gonna do what they want to do, I'll do what I have to do too. Screw them. That's what I believe in now. So this is my advice to you, Lynette: at the end of the day, just look out for yourself and screw everyone else.'

★

Kenny was in his mother's bed watching *Toy Story 3* on the portable DVD player. Lynette sat next to him and watched it until it ended and then she helped him up and made sure he used the toilet and brushed his teeth. She helped him on with his pyjamas and got him under the covers of his mother's bed and turned off the bedside lamp, leaving only two Superman nightlights shining from nearby outlets.

She sat on the bed next to him and held his hand. 'I have no idea about Mona's place,' she said gently. 'I've never been there so I don't know. But I got a bad feeling it's not going to be very nice there. But I don't want you to worry, Kenny, because I'm going to come back and get you when I'm settled. I promise. I really do promise. It might take me a bit but I'll find a place that I can own, and maybe I really will own a bakery. Maybe in St Louis or Kansas City or Cleveland, like Shirley said, or maybe in some smaller town that's just cheaper. And when I get there I won't mess around, Kenny. I won't. I swear I won't. I won't let myself get depressed. And I won't get mean or bitter. I won't be cruel. And I'll try hard and I'll make sure the darkness doesn't get me. I'll try my hardest to make sure it doesn't. You'll see . . . I'll remember to be kind and I'll try not to be so weak. I'll try to be strong. And I'll think about you every minute and I'll love you every second. Thanks for saving me, Kenny. Thanks for being my brother.' She kissed him on the face, over and over, until he pulled his head away and pushed her off him. Tears were streaming down her face. 'Remember to say hello to the Trail Blazers for me. Tell them not to trade CJ or Damian. And remember, no matter where you end up, I'll come and get you. I swear on my life I will, and when you see me I'll be good, I'll be doing good.'

★

The things she put in her car weren't much: clothes, a lamp Jack had bought her, a wristwatch of her grandfather's and two boxes of dishes her grandmother had left her. All of it fit in the trunk of the Buick. The TV in the living room was on but her mother was asleep on the couch. Lynette made a pot of coffee and waited for it to brew. When it had she filled her thermos and went back out to her mother. She sat on the edge of the couch, pushed softly on her shoulder, but her mother wouldn't wake. The pint of gin and the cup she was drinking from were empty.

At the kitchen table Lynette wrote a note to her mother saying goodbye and that she loved her. When she'd locked the front door, she put her key through the mail slot and got in the Buick. She poured a cup of coffee and started the car. It was still raining and past midnight when she got on the Interstate and headed east.

Acknowledgements

I'd like to thank my gal Lee, who put up with me while I built and rebuilt and rebuilt this novel. For a short book it sure took a long time. So thank you, Lee. You're the best of the best. And Lesley Thorne, my great friend and agent, for sticking with me all these years. Also Angus Cargill at Faber & Faber for being so damn smart and such a great editor. I'd also like to thank Silvia Crompton, Andrew Benbow, Josh Smith, Katie Hall, Libby Marshall, Josephine Salverda and all the fine people at Faber & Faber for helping bring my books to life.

When I moved to Portland I was twenty-six years old. After years of working in warehouses, I began a ten-year stint as a house painter and started a band called Richmond Fontaine. Sean Oldham, the drummer, was called HQ because he was the smartest and most successful. He and his wife owned their home. He even had a passport. One day I drove him to a derelict 480-square-foot house that was for sale. It was on a busy street next to a mini-mart but in a good neighbourhood. I told him it was my dream to buy it and he said I'd be an idiot not to try. I had no confidence in myself but I was raised to believe that success was owning your own home. Over the course of fifteen years I saved twenty thousand dollars for a down payment, and I bought the derelict house for seventy-two thousand dollars in 2000. Portland then was a city full of beautiful houses that working-class people could afford to buy. It seems like a dream now.

My life changed when I bought that house. I quit going out so much, I began taking better care of myself, I mowed my lawn, I bought a semi-new couch and a brand-new colour TV and a *Better Homes and Gardens* cookbook. I began to like myself. I want to thank the Rose City for giving me a home and a chance when for a lot of my life I didn't know there was a chance to be had.